Augustus Thomas

Arizona

A drama in four acts

Augustus Thomas

Arizona
A drama in four acts

ISBN/EAN: 9783337105495

Printed in Europe, USA, Canada, Australia, Japan

Cover: Foto ©Andreas Hilbeck / pixelio.de

More available books at **www.hansebooks.com**

"I can never tell you exactly the way I felt."

ARIZONA

A Drama in Four Acts

By AUGUSTUS THOMAS, *Author of* ALABAMA, IN MIZZOURA, etc., etc. ∴ ∴ ∴

New York: R. H. Russell
M DCCC XCIX

The PERSONS of the PLAY

The ORIGINAL CAST at
Hamlin's Grand Opera House, Chicago

HENRY CANBY, owner of Aravaipa ranch,
MR. THEODORE ROBERTS

Colonel BONHAM, Eleventh United States
Cavalry, ... MR. EDWIN HOLT

SAM WONG, a cook, . . . MR. STEPHEN FRENCH

Mrs. CANBY, wife of the rancher, . MISS MATTIE EARLE

ESTRELLA BONHAM, wife of the Colonel, MISS MABEL BERT

LENA KELLAR, a waitress, . . MISS ADORA ANDREWS

Lieutenant DENTON, Eleventh United
States Cavalry, ... MR. ROBERT EDESON

BONITA CANBY, Estrella's sister, . . MISS OLIVE MAY

Miss MacCULLAGH, a school teacher, MISS EDITH ATHELSTONE

Dr. FENLON, surgeon, Eleventh United States
Cavalry, ... MR. SAMUEL EDWARDS

Captain HODGMAN, Eleventh United
States Cavalry, ... MR. ARTHUR BYRON

TONY MOSTANO, a vaquero, . . MR. VINCENT SERRANO

Lieutenant HALLOCK, Eleventh United
States Cavalry, . . . MR. FRANKLIN GARLAND

Sergeant KELLAR, Eleventh United States
Cavalry, ... MR. WALTER HALE

Lieutenant YOUNG, Eleventh United
States Cavalry. . . . MR. LIONEL BARRYMORE

Major COCHRAN, Eleventh United States
Cavalry, ... MR. MENIFEE JOHNSTONE

ARIZONA

THE FIRST ACT

*HE* scene represents the interior of an adobe courtyard, and shows three sides of a rectangle formed by the dwelling-house and stables of a well-to-do rancher. On the right of the stage three doors open upon a small hooded and latticed veranda; the doors leading respectively to the dining, living, and bedrooms of the dwelling. On the left of the stage are the stables and wagon-sheds, through the doors of which show the mangers. A Mexican carette protrudes from the wagon-shed. Near the stable and at the back is a well, with an adobe curb. The third and back side of the rectangle is filled by a large gateway, which may be closed by two massive wooden gates, now standing open. Through the open gateway, and over the low roof of the dwelling and stable, the mountains that wall in the

Aravaipa Valley show in bold relief against the hot summer sky of Arizona. HENRY CANBY, *the ranch owner, aged sixty, and* COLONEL BONHAM, *aged fifty-two, are seated at a rough deal table. Julep glasses are beside them. Both men are in their shirt-sleeves.*

CANBY.

[*As* COLONEL *draws last of julep through straw.*] Have another?

COLONEL.

No, I think not.

CANBY.

Well, if you only *think* not— [*Calls.*] Sam—

COLONEL.

They 're just a trifle strong for me.

[SAM, *a Chinaman, enters from the house.*

CANBY.

Sam, fix two more of these, and don't put quite so much whiskey in the Colonel's.

SAM.

Yes sa. [*He goes into the house carrying the julep glasses.*

COLONEL.

I really oughtn't to take another *one*, but it's been a year since I had a *smell* of mint.

CANBY.

I'll do up a bundle of it for you.

COLONEL.

No, no, I couldn't use it at the Post.

CANBY.

Well, if you can't find a market for a bundle of mint in a regiment of cavalry, I'd like to know where on God's green earth—

COLONEL.

Oh, they'd *like* it all right, but it's a bad example in a Colonel. Besides Estrella kicks if I get off the water-wagon too often. Once she said this nose of mine commenced to get little blue railroad maps ; had to paint it with bismuth. And if Estrella scents liquor, anywhere, she pretends they're coming back again.

CANBY.

I know Estrella. Used to try to put a crimp in my medicine with the same scare; but I pretended to like it, and used to shine up my horn this way [*He catches his nose with one hand and pretends to polish it vigorously with the other.*] whenever she began her lecture.

COLONEL.

I reckon you'd toe out a little more, if you were her husband.

CANBY.

Yes, I guess I would. A woman that's married to a fellow has a pretty tight cinch on him—that is, if he likes her.

COLONEL.

And I confess I do like Estrella. She's really great, Governor. You're her father, of course, and ought to know her, but she's a brick.

CANBY.

Colonel, at her age they're all pretty good—and when one of 'em happens to marry a man that's sort o' settled—

COLONEL.

Or even gray-headed—

CANBY.

Yes—why he 's pretty sure to be a little dotty about her.

COLONEL.

You think I'm " dotty " about Estrella ?

CANBY.

[*In an explosive high laugh.*] He, he— Oh, no—

COLONEL.

Well, how do I show it ?

CANBY.

Why, ridin' down here. Why didn't you stay with the troop, and come to-day ?

COLONEL.

I avoided the heat.

CANBY.

[*Resignedly.*] All right. [SAM *re-enters with the juleps.*] Come on. There 's yours.

[SAM *places the glasses on the table and goes into the house.*]

COLONEL.

[*Taking his glass.*] Well, that 's a fact.

CANBY.

I s'pose if Estrella hadn't been here, you'd 'a' rode down jest the same.

COLONEL.

No, I don't say that.

CANBY.

You' d been a week at Carlos, and you was simply honin' like a sailor to get back,—and, Colonel, you *are* jes' naturally dotty about her.

HENRY CANBY

COLONEL.

[*Moodily.*] You don't understand, Governor.

CANBY.

[*Laughing again.*] He, he! Well, you 're startin' a little late to learn me. He, he!

COLONEL.

I 'm rather careful about Estrella—[*He rises and looks cautiously about.*]—because—there's something wrong.

CANBY.

Wrong ?

COLONEL.

She ain't happy.

CANBY.

Git out.

COLONEL.

I mean it.

CANBY.

She 's been here a whole week, and I never saw her chipperer in her life.

COLONEL.

But—I was away.

CANBY.

Well ? [*The* COLONEL *shrugs shoulders.*] You mean that *made* her chipper ?

COLONEL.

[*Sitting.*] Yes.

CANBY.

Why ?

COLONEL.

Because she isn't happy at the Post.

CANBY.

Well, you ain't the Post.

COLONEL.

But I'm her husband.

CANBY.

[*After a pause.*] Ain't the julep brewed proper?

COLONEL.

[*Taking the julep mechanically.*] I'd think, maybe, she was lonesome for her own people, but most of her life was spent away from you, at school and at the Seminary in 'Frisco.

CANBY.

[*Rising and walking.*] Colonel, I've broke a good many colts, broke lots of 'em to go double. When you first yoke 'em up, they jes' whip-saw that way. [*He pantomimes a sudden and disconcerted pulling with his hands.*] They ain't never both agin the tugs at the same time. Then I give 'em the gaff, an' after they've run 'emselves nearly to a standstill, I point 'em home. They come back together like the wheelers in a band wagon.

COLONEL.

But I'm no colt, Governor.

CANBY.

You are at gittin' married; and all new married folks are jes' the same. For a while whip-saw—then bolt. Some bolt harder and more of it than others, but they bolt—all of 'em.

COLONEL.

Well, are Estrella and I whip-sawing or bolting?

CANBY.

[*Resuming his place at the table.*] I take it you 're boltin'. Each of you thinks, if he could only run a little faster, he'd get away from the other ; but you can't. You 're yoked. Now, that don't mean trouble ; it simply means you ain't used to your harness.

[MRS. CANBY *enters excitedly from the house, carrying a pair of field glasses.*]

MRS. CANBY.

Henry.

CANBY.

Hello, mother.

MRS. CANBY.

I been lookin' at that cavalry troop through the Colonel's spy-glasses.

CANBY.

Ma *loves* the soldiers.

MRS. CANBY.

Git out! I been watchin' fur Bonita.

CANBY.

Oh, Bonita 's all right.

MRS. CANBY.

She went out at three, and it 's after six now.

CANBY.

Well ?

MRS. CANBY.

And jest as I thought, she 's gallivanted up the Valley to meet the troop.

CANBY.

Well, we ain't never hung anybody for that.

MRS. CANBY.

But one girl herdin' with forty soldiers all afternoon—

COLONEL.

Why, bless your soul, mother, she 's Estrella's sister, and any one of them would let Bonita walk on him.

MRS. CANBY.

I don't see that helps any. Imagine her walkin' on one of 'em. [*Goes anxiously to the gate.*]

CANBY.

Colonel, Ma won't stand for any poetry.

MRS. CANBY.

I was a girl in this territory myself. [*She returns.*]

CANBY.

Well, nothing happened to *you*, that you couldn't get over, did they?

MRS. CANBY.

[*After a glare at him.*] Well, I 'll leave it to anybody that knows you. [CANBY *begins to polish his nose.*] Stop that! [CANBY *stops.*] Whenever he begins that tom-fool dido, you kin know Henry 's had his full gauge.

CANBY.

Colonel, she always jackets me when either of the girls steps over a trace.

MRS. CANBY.

Well, somebody 's responsible.

CANBY.

See? Ma 's made out somehow that it 's my fault they was n't boys.

MRS. CANBY.

Where 's Estrella ?

CANBY.

Layin' down.

MRS. CANBY.

Well, I think she might be doin' better when the Colonel 's rode nearly all night to spend the day with her.

COLONEL.

Oh no, no.   Estrella usually takes a nap in the afternoon at the Post.

> [ESTRELLA *enters from the house dressed in an easy wrapper.*

ESTRELLA.

[*Half sleepily.*]   Hello, everybody.

MRS. CANBY.

Are you up for all day, Estrella?

ESTRELLA.

Yes, and all night, if it 's as pretty as last night was.   [*She puts her arms over the* COLONEL's *shoulders and kisses him.*

COLONEL.

Get a nap, sweetheart ?

ESTRELLA.

Not much.   I was reading most of the time.   Has C Troop come ?

COLONEL.

Not yet.

MRS. CANBY.

[*From the gateway.*]   They 're in sight, and Bonita 's Joan-of-Arc-in' 'em.

ESTRELLA.

Oh, that's fun. I'd have gone with her if I 'd known it. [*She pauses as she catches sight of the glasses.*] What are you drinking, Frank?

COLONEL.

Julep. [*Glances warningly at* CANBY.

ESTRELLA.

You mustn't let Pa get you into bad habits.
[CANBY *begins polishing nose.*

MRS. CANBY.

Stop it.

CANBY.

We been drowndin' our sorrows, the Colonel and me. He 's got an idear, Estrella, that you ain't easy down at the Post.

ESTRELLA.

Why, I don't see how.

COLONEL.

[*Putting his arm about her waist.*] Thought you were a trifle moody, that 's all. Thought maybe you were getting a little homesick for the city.

ESTRELLA.

[*In lulling manner.*] Why, no.

MRS. CANBY.

Well, any woman that could get lonesome at the Post, deserves it. Huh! You ought to have a dose of this place—cactus and sand, and slab-sided cattle, and havin' to let the clock run down to tell when it 's Sunday. I don't know what women want now-a-days. [*She goes up to the gate.*

COLONEL.

Maybe they want their husbands like C Troop's first Lieutenant, young and handsome——

ESTRELLA.

[*Her fingers over his lips.*] Stop—stop, I won't hear you!

COLONEL.

And then, as soon as I 'd got her, I log-rolled a transfer down here in the desert, where she can't possibly escape.

CANBY.

Don't call the Aravaipa Valley a desert, Colonel.

COLONEL.

Estrella called it that.

ESTRELLA.

But I didn't know how pretty Fort Grant could be. I thought it was all like this.

COLONEL.

Oh, the Post is better than this, but it isn't San Francisco, is it, dear?

ESTRELLA.

I don't think of San Francisco, Frank.

MRS. CANBY.

I hope not. San Francisco 's got all it can answer for. You ain't been anything but faint-and-fall-in-it, and Bonita wouldn't touch a darnin' bag with a ten foot pole since they San Franciscoed her.

CANBY.

Well, what 's the money for, Ma, if it ain't white bread to the girls?

Mrs. Canby.

Well, it might be a little white bread to me.

Canby.

[*To* Colonel.] Woundn't you think it was nothin' but crackers and water ? An' she 's got finery enough in those rooms to sink a ship. They 's a dymond breast-pin, big as a paddle-lock—a gold bracelet so thick that the greasers don't steal it, 'cause they think it 's brass. There 's silk dresses ——

Mrs. Canby.

Yes, and greasers are all they are to show 'em to. I never been out, Colonel, in my breast-pin but once in five years, and that was to the opera at El Paso.

Canby.

Oh, Ma, you wore it on the sleepin'-car to Phœnix!

Mrs. Canby.

But *we* was the only folks in the car, besides the nigger.

Canby.

Well, I saw him looking at it.

[Lena *enters from the house.*

Lena.

Mrs. Canby.

Mrs. Canby.

Yes ?

[*The* Colonel *rises from his chair.*

Lena.

The troop is up to the fence now—they 're just coming through the gate, double column.

COLONEL.

[*Brightly.*]   How are you, Lena?

LENA.

[*Moodily.*]   Well, thank you, Colonel.

COLONEL.

Shake hands.   [*He takes her hand.*

LENA.

[*Embarrassed little laugh.*]   Huh—   [*She goes quickly into the house.*

COLONEL.

[*Looking after Lena.*]   All right, now?

MRS. CANBY.

[*Sullenly.*]   Not strong enough to do much work.   She's kind of a lady's maid for Bonita.

COLONEL.

Too bad, isn't it?   She'd 'a' made some chap a good wife.

CANBY.

[*Optimistically.*]   In Arizona, my boy, she's worth a whole hatful of *dead* ones yet.

COLONEL.

Well, there's C Troop.   I'll put on my blouse.

[*He goes into the house.*

MRS. CANBY.

Henry!

CANBY.

Well?

MRS. CANBY.

You put on *your* coat, too.

CANBY.

Why ?   They don't have to salute me.

MRS. CANBY.

It don't look decent, with Bonita around, and those young fellows.

CANBY.

[*Going.*]   You bet, Ma.   Every day is Sunday when the soldiers come.   [*He goes into the house.*

MRS. CANBY.

And now, Estrella, stop your mopin'.   You 've made your bed, and you 've got to sleep in it.

ESTRELLA.

Did I make it ?

MRS. CANBY.

[*Aggressively.*]   Yes, you did.   You could 'a' had most any man in California—in the army, or out of it.

ESTRELLA.

What about Thompson ?

MRS. CANBY.

He was fast !   That 's what—fast.

ESTRELLA.

[*Shrugs shoulders.*]   And a row, wasn't there, when young Burgess began calling.

MRS. CANBY.

He was all upper lip, and no chin, like a prairie dog.

ESTRELLA.

[*Wearily.*]   Oh, yes, all wrong some way, but the Colonel.

M R S. C A N B Y.

Well, I leave it to you, wasn't he the best of 'em—the whole kit and boodle ?

E S T R E L L A.

Do I say he wasn't.

[*The sound of many horses on a dirt road and a jingle of sabres begins faintly and grows in volume.*

M R S. C A N B Y.

You act like it, I must say.   And he notices it, too.   He rode nearly all night to get here, and the way you appreciate it, is to *sleep* all day.

E S T R E L L A.

Well, the troop will be here to-night, and we 'll be up late.

[*The light begins to change to the golden yellow of an Arizona sunset.*

· M R S. C A N B Y.

Why ? Your Pa an' me will do the entertainin'.   You can go to bed.   Jes' you don't fret so much about the troop ; and while we 're about it, Estrella, let 's understand each other.   There must be no goin's-on, this time, with this Captain Hodgman—here.

E S T R E L L A.

That talk bores me, Mother, excessively.

M R S. C A N B Y.

Well, I make it jest the same.

E S T R E L L A.

You 're flighty about Captain Hodgman, and the Colonel 's always harping on Mr. Denton.   [*She goes up to gate.*

M RS. CANBY.

You 've got the best man in the regiment, the boss of all of 'em, and so don't get frisky with the others. [HODGMAN's *voice is heard outside.*

H ODGMAN.

[*Outside the court.*] Right into line—

[COLONEL *re-enters from the house in uniform.*

COLONEL.

[*To* ESTRELLA, *who is at the gate.*] How do the fellows look, dearie ?

H ODGMAN.

[*Outside.*] Halt.

ESTRELLA.

Very well.

[*The general noise quickly quiets and out of it grows the crescendo approach of two horses racing.*

M RS. CANBY.

[*Angrily.*] Now, look at that ! Bonita 's a perfect harum-scarum whenever that fellow 's around. [*Calls.*] Bonita ! Bonita ! Stop it. [*Horses slow down. Laughter by* BONITA *and* DENTON.

[DENTON *enters in service uniform, and covered with dust.*

D ENTON.

Mr. Canby here ? Colonel! [*Salutes. The* COLONEL *returns* DENTON's *salute.*] Captain Hodgman's compliments, wants to know where to make camp.

M RS. CANBY.

Why, the same old field.

DENTON.

But the home cattle—

MRS. CANBY.

Our boys 'll turn them out.

DENTON.

Thank you. [*He again salutes the* COLONEL, *who salutes in answer.* DENTON, *turning to go, meets* BONITA *laughing and leading her horse, from which she has just dismounted. He smilingly whispers to her and disappears.*

MRS. CANBY.

Well, Miss, it 's about time.

> [*A cowboy takes* BONITA's *horse and leads it away to left back of the gate.*

BONITA.

Why, Mother, it isn't sun-down.

> [CANBY *comes from the house with coat on, and hair combed sleek.*

CANBY.

[*Smoothing his front.*] Well, we're ready for 'em, Mother.

> [BONITA *comes down.*

HODGMAN.

[*Outside.*] Dismount.

> [CANBY *goes to the well, puts one foot on the curb and arranges his trousers over his boot.*

BONITA.

Colonel, I scouted C Troop in from Curry's wind mills.

COLONEL.

All right. I'll put you on the pay rolls.

BONITA.

Miss MacCullagh 's with the troop, and Ma—we 've planned for me to go to the Post with Miss MacCullagh and Estrella.

MRS. CANBY.

Not with this C Troop there.

COLONEL.

Why ?

MRS. CANBY.

Bonita 's a little too frisky with this First Lieutenant

BONITA.

Why, ma !

COLONEL.

Denton ?

MRS. CANBY.

Yes, Denton

COLONEL.

[*Smiling.*] Well, Denton 's a splendid fellow. Isn't he, Estrella ?

[ESTRELLA *turns away, annoyed.* CANBY *who has come down right meets her back of the table.*

MRS. CANBY.

I know about him. They ain't a piece of deviltry in the Valley, he ain't in it. An' when he 's around, Bonita, she 's like a calf in a prairie fire.

[BONITA *prances comically up to the carette.*

COLONEL.

Oh, boy's fun. . Denton ? Why, Bonita, Denton 's the best cavalryman that ever stood in the saddle.

[*Enter* HODGMAN, *throngh the gate from right. He is in service uniform and very dusty.*

HODGMAN.

[*Salutes* COLONEL. *The* COLONEL *salutes in answer. Bows to others who return his bow.*

CANBY AND MRS. CANBY.

Evening, Captain.

HODGMAN.

Came through all right, sir ; men and horses in good condition. Doctor Fenlon and school teacher just behind in the ambulance.

COLONEL.

Very well, Captain. Let the men make camp and get supper, have everything ready in the morning, to start sharply at eight.

[HODGMAN *and* COLONEL *exchange salutes.*

CANBY.

Colonel, officers in here.

HODGMAN.

[*Who has started off.*] No need to trouble, Mr. Canby, we have our tents.

COLONEL.

Oh, come in. It pleases Mr. Canby and his wife.

MRS. CANBY.

Yes, indeed.

HODGMAN.

Thank you.

CANBY.

Supper !

HODGMAN.

[*From the gateway.*] I 'll see the troops disposed first. [*Salutes the* COLONEL.] Ambulance, sir.

VOICE.

[*Outside.*] Whoa.

COLONEL.

All right. [HODGMAN *disappears. Noise of ambulance brake and stop is heard outside with jingle of chains.*

[ESTRELLA *goes to gate.*

BONITA.

Colonel—you make Ma let me visit the Post.

[LENA *re-enters.*

COLONEL.

Of course.

[Miss MacCULLAGH *and* DOCTOR FENLON *come into gateway. They are very travel-stained.*

ESTRELLA.

Miss MacCullagh, my mother and father.

[CANBY *bows.*

MRS. CANBY.

How are you ? [*Shakes hands and kisses her.*] Doctor, glad to see you. [*Takes bag from* MISS MACCULLAGH, *hands it to* LENA.] Now, you poor thing, come right to your room. I 'll lock the bath-room door on my side, and you can git right in it.

[*Bustles effusively into the house followed by* MISS MAC- CULLAGH *and* LENA *with the bag.*

CANBY.

Sit down, Doctor, and rest yourself.

DOCTOR.

[*Who has been limbering his knees.*] Mr. Canby, I shall *never* sit down again.

COLONEL.

[*Laughing.*] Been in the ambulance since daylight.

DOCTOR.

You know, that school teacher 's one of the nicest girls I ever saw, Colonel—not a bit *like* a school teacher ; blushes, you know, and all that. [*Re-enter* LENA *with bag.*

COLONEL.

I hope you didn't make her blush, Doctor.

LENA.

[*To* ESTRELLA.] Mrs. Bonham, that lady says this ain't her bag.

ESTRELLA.

Where did you get it ?

DOCTOR.

[*Looking at similar bag in his hand.*] Nobody said it was her bag. Lena, that 's mine. [*Takes bag from* LENA ; *holds both.*] You 're looking better. [*Regards her professionally.* LENA *is embarrassed and goes into the house carrying the second bag.*] The idea of mistaking my New York Russia leather bag for this miserable Kansas City affair.

BONITA.

[*Laughs and goes toward house.*] Doctor, your room is just through this hall.

DOCTOR.

[*Going.*]   Thank you.

BONITA.

You and Mr. Denton will be together.

DOCTOR.

[*Pausing.*]   Pardon me, but I can't sleep with another *man*.

CANBY.

Two beds.

DOCTOR.

Oh, easy enough.   [*Goes into house.*

CANBY.

[*Calling after him.*]   Supper soon as you 're ready.   Don't
keep it waiting, girls.

ESTRELLA.

[*Going.*]   You ready, Colonel ?

COLONEL.

[*Looking himself over and smiling.*]   Well, what else ?   Epaul-
ettes ?

ESTRELLA.

All right.   [*She goes into house.*

CANBY.

Come, Colonel.   [*Disappears with Colonel through door to
dining-room.*

[*BONITA goes to the gate, meets HODGMAN and HAL-
LOCK, with strikers carrying packs.   They give way,
smiling.   BONITA goes through gate, but remains
in view, looking off.   HODGMAN, HALLOCK and two
strikers enter the court.*

HODGMAN.

Same room, Mr. Hallock.   [LENA *re-enters from house.*

HALLOCK.

This way.   [*Exit, followed by two strikers.*

LENA.

Miss Bonita.

HODGMAN.

Lena. [*Looks furtively back toward* BONITA, *who is not regarding him.*

LENA.

[*Shrinking from him with disgust.*]   No.

HODGMAN.

Don't be foolish, Lena. You see, the trouble 's all over, and you 've got a nice place here. I told you I 'd do something handsome for you, if you kept still, and I will.

LENA.

I kept still because I didn't want my father to kill you.

[DENTON *appears in gateway with* BONITA.

HODGMAN.

Ha! ha! ha! You wait till Christmas. [*Chucks* LENA *under the chin and goes into house laughing.*

[BONITA *comes down with* DENTON.

[*The yellow sunlight deepens.*

DENTON.

I understand your father 's going to put us up again.

B O N I T A.

Yes, you 're with the Doctor—in there.   [*To* LENA.]   In a
minute.   [LENA *goes into house.*

   [QUIGLEY *enters gate with* DENTON'S *pack.*

D E N T O N.

[*Seeing broom.*] I 'll leave some of this real estate outside. [*He
hands broom to* QUIGLEY, *who brushes him.* BONITA *retreats down
right centre.*]   Careful, Quigley [*as broom strikes back of neck*].
Little sunburnt there.   Thanks !

   [QUIGLEY *takes* DENTON'S *pack into house.*

D E N T O N.

[*Alone with* BONITA.]   Well, what about the visit to the
Post ?

B O N I T A.

Ma hasn't decided yet.

D E N T O N.

I 'll speak to her about it.

B O N I T A.

[*Alarmed.*]   Oh, no!

   [TONY, *a Mexican vaquero, enters from stable, carrying
      a horse bucket.*

D E N T O N.

[*To* BONITA.]   No ? [*To* TONY.]   Hello, Tony.   [TONY
nods with a pleased grin.

B O N I T A.

You, 'Tenant, must pretend not to care about it.

"'Things are so much nicer in your room.'"

DENTON.

I must?

[HODGMAN's *and* HALLOCK's *strikers return from house and pass out through the gate.*]

BONITA.

Well, *all* the gentlemen.

DENTON.

Oh! [TONY *has filled his bucket from the well and started to go.*] That a horse bucket?

TONY.

Yes, sir.

DENTON.

That 'll do me. [TONY *sets the bucket down.*]

BONITA.

[*As* DENTON *kneels over bucket washing his hands.*] Why, things are so much nicer in your room.

DENTON.

[*Pausing.*] Er—a—I like the scenery. [*Smiles—buries face in bucket.*]

BONITA.

[*Also smiling, calls.*] Oh! Lena. [*As if seeing her.*] A towel, please, for Mr. Denton.

DENTON.

Oh, I don't need a towel, Miss Bonita. What do you think I carry a handkerchief for? [*Stands up.*]

[QUIGLEY *returns from house.*]

QUIGLEY.

[*Saluting.*] That all, sir? [*Re-enter* LENA *carrying a towel.*]

DENTON.

That 's all, Quigley.   Thanks.   [QUIGLEY *goes out at gate.*

DENTON.

[*Taking towel.*]   Hello, Lena, glad to see you.   Got your
Dad with us, too.

BONITA.

But your hair.

DENTON.

Look bad ?

BONITA.

[*Nodding.*]   'm 'm—that is—not very.

DENTON.

Oh—lend me a side-comb.   [BONITA *nods*—DENTON *hands towel*
to LENA.]   Thank you.   [*Goes to* BONITA.
    [TONY *starts left with bucket.*
    [SERGEANT KELLAR *enters at gate.*

KELLAR.

Why, Lena !   [TONY *turns at sound of* LENA'S *name.* LENA *goes*
to KELLAR *and kisses him.*

TONY.

[*Fiercely.*]   Who is this man ?   [*All but* KELLAR *look at* TONY.]
You !   You !   [KELLAR *looks at* TONY.]   Who are *you* ?

LENA.

This is my father.
    [TONY *quickly disappears into stable carrying bucket, while*
    DENTON, BONITA *and* LENA *laugh at him.*

KELLAR.

[*Saluting.*]   'Tenant.   Stables—

ARIZONA

DENTON.

[*Returning salute.*] Very well. I'll be right out. [KELLAR *goes to gate.*

KELLAR.

'Tenant. [*Salutes.*

DENTON.

[*Saluting.*] Sergeant?

KELLAR.

Who is dat man?

BONITA.

That's one of the vaqueros.

KELLAR.

[*Looking after* TONY.] Ferricht!
[*He goes out through gateway.* LENA, *suppressing a laugh, disappears into stable.*

DENTON.

[*Returning comb to* BONITA.] I have to go now.
[*He starts up toward gate.*

BONITA.

Where?

DENTON.

Stables inspection.

BONITA.

But supper's ready.

DENTON.

[*Pausing in gateway.*] I'm afraid I'll be a little late to it, then.

BONITA.

[*Also going, but toward house.*] I, too.

DENTON.

[*Turning with complimentary eagerness.*]   Eh!

BONITA.

Must change my dress.

DENTON.

Oh!   [*A pause and a negotiating approach.*]   Take me about fifteen minutes with the horses.

BONITA.

Take me about fifteen minutes to dress.   [*She in turn takes a step toward* DENTON *with challenging diffidence.*

DENTON.

Make us *both* late, won't it?

> [LENA *re-enters from the stable and gets mandolin from lattice.*

BONITA.

Yes.   What 's that, Lena?

LENA.

Tony's.   [*She holds mandolin up to view.*

BONITA.

Very well.

> [LENA *carries mandolin into the stable.*

DENTON.

Miss Bonita, do you know the most exciting thing that 's happened to me since I 've been in Arizona?

> [*Yellow sunlight begins changing to red.*

BONITA.

What?

DENTON.

That side comb.

BONITA.

This side comb?

DENTON.

Yes.

[BONITA *sits on the end of the table.* DENTON *follows with portentous intensity.*

BONITA.

[*With feminine dissembling.*] Why! It 's like any other side comb. May be a little more curved.

DENTON.

[*Lightly, but not misled.*] Well, perhaps that 's it. Funny, though, to run up against a new curve, 'way out here.

BONITA.

I don't know what you 're talking about. [*She smiles in complete confusion.*

DENTON.

Well—I don't know that *I* do. [*He walks away satisfied with his skirmish, then resumes deliberately.*] That comb— [*Pause.*] I 've combed my own hair ever since my mother quit brushing it round a broom handle. [*Pantomime of curling hair and pause.*] I 've used all kinds of combs—combs just fresh from the drug store, and smelling like cologne—I 've used combs that were chained alongside of roller-towels—used *every* kind, I guess. [*Parenthetically.*] And I asked you for *that* one more in fun than anything else— [*He approaches her with voice lowered to an ardent tremolo and speaks with his face close over her shoulder.*] but I never can tell you just exactly the way I felt when I used it.

[TONY'S *mandolin is heard playing " The Crescent Moon."*

BONITA.

[*After pause, during which she turns to him with some amusement not unmixed with alarm.*] You 're a funny fellow.

DENTON.

[*Looking into her eyes.*] Am I?

BONITA.

[*Slowly retreating half a step.*] Yes.

> [DENTON *follows her almost imperceptibly. There is a moment's pause, during which there is no adequate explanation for his not kissing her. Both sigh, and* DENTON *recovers with a step or two to the rear.*]

DENTON.

You know, at the Post, most of us bachelors have quarters in the same building.

BONITA.

Yes, I know that. [*Very matter-of-fact.*

DENTON.

After being together a while, we become rather free with one another's possessions. It's a way we get into in the Academy. But, if we don't like a chap pretty well, [*In a tone of judicial punishment.*] we don't use his things. [*Pause.*] Now, how do girls feel about that?

BONITA.

[*With Alice-in-Wonderland manner.*] I don't think they know about it. Has it been ~~printed?~~ *published* ⸰

DENTON.

[*Menacingly.*] I mean, among themselves. Is the *mine* and *thine* rather sharply drawn? [*He comes to her, his wooing resumed.*

BONITA.

Yes, [*She turns, meeting his gaze with insinuating frankness. Pause.*] unless *they* like a fellow.

DENTON.

[*Laughing nervously.*] Oh! Kind o' human, after all.

BONITA.

[*Also laughing.*] At times, yes.

DENTON.

[*In playful earnestness.*] Any other fellow ever used *that* comb ?

> [BONITA *shakes her head, and* DENTON *smiles and turns away much pleased.*

BONITA.

[*Taking comb from hair and regarding it.*] I haven't had it very long.

DENTON.

Oh ! [*Pause.*] And I suppose there aren't very *many* fellows passing this way ?

BONITA.

[*With affected innocence.*] No, not many.

DENTON.

[*Reflecting.*] Well, that rather cuts down my average— still— [*Pause.*

BONITA.

What ?

DENTON.

Do me a favor ?

BONITA.

Yes.

DENTON.

[*Really serious and very near her.*] *Don't* lend it to any other. [*Pause*] Will you ? [BONITA *purses lips in restraint of smile, and slowly shakes her head.*] Thank you.

> [DENTON *smiles and turns with sigh of relief.*

B O N I T A.

[*Taking second comb from her hair.*] It 's pretty hard, though, to tell them apart.

D E N T O N.

[*Quickly.*]   I mean both.

B O N I T A.

Both ! !

D E N T O N.

Both. [*Positively.* BONITA *sighs with resignation, sits slowly and replaces combs.*]   Thank you.   [*Starts up.*]   Fifteen minutes.
[TONY'S *mandolin ceases playing.*

B O N I T A.

[*Quickly.*]   Mr. Denton.

D E N T O N.

[*Turning.*]   Yes.
[*The red sunset shows a glow of purple.*

B O N I T A.

[*Pause.*]   You—you 've been around the country a good deal, haven't you ?

D E N T O N.

Quite a bit, yes.

B O N I T A.

[*Archly.*]   Have you tied up very many side combs ?

D E N T O N.

[*Meaningly.*]   My first pair.   [BONITA *moves one step down.*]
'Tisn't going to be too hard, is it ?   [BONITA *looks at him and, without answering, goes to the table.* DENTON *follows.   Her face is averted; and he leans on the table speaking over her right shoulder.*]
You see, in this cattle-law country, some fellows rope the first

pretty creature they see, and call her all theirs; I'm asking only a little loyalty in the matter of side combs. Then, if that doesn't fret her—why—[*He restrains a manifested impulse to embrace her, reverently kisses a lock of her hair and with a sigh runs quickly off. A bell rings.* BONITA *follows to gate looking after him. The* DOCTOR, MISS MACCULLAGH *and* MRS. CANBY *enter from house and come down.*

DOCTOR.
[*To* MISS MACCULLAGH.] Feel refreshed?

MISS MACCULLAGH.
Yes, indeed. [DOCTOR *indicates door to dining-room for* MISS MACCULLAGH.

MRS. CANBY.
Why, Bonita, you ain't ready.

[MISS MACCULLAGH *goes into dining-room.*

BONITA.
I'm not hungry, Ma.

MRS. CANBY.
[*Going with the* DOCTOR.] I wish you'd give her something for that, Doctor; the soldiers excite her so.

DOCTOR.
I'll give her a soldier.

MRS. CANBY.
Git out!

DOCTOR.
Best *I* can do. [*Goes into dining-room followed by* MRS. CANBY.
[HALLOCK *enters and goes into dining-room.*

HODGMAN.
[*Entering and looking about.*] Oh—Miss Canby, that was supper bell, wasn't it?

BONITA.

Yes.

HODGMAN.

Going in ?

BONITA.

Not just yet, I must change my dress. [*She comes down from the gateway.*

HODGMAN.

Can't improve on that. [BONITA *smiles, and bows a " thank you."*] Who taught you to ride, Miss Bonita ?

BONITA.

Pa says I was able to ride before I could walk. Anybody in Arizona who can't ride a horse, had better be dead. [*Laughs.*

HODGMAN.

Well, if riding is the test, you 've a good long life ahead of *you.*

BONITA.

Not in Arizona, I hope.

HODGMAN.

You don't like it ?

BONITA. .

Do you ?

HODGMAN.

[*Smiling.*] I have to.

BONITA.

Oh ! well, *I* have to—for a while, anyway.

HODGMAN.

[*With apprehensive look back.*] Made any plans for escape ? [*Lightly.*

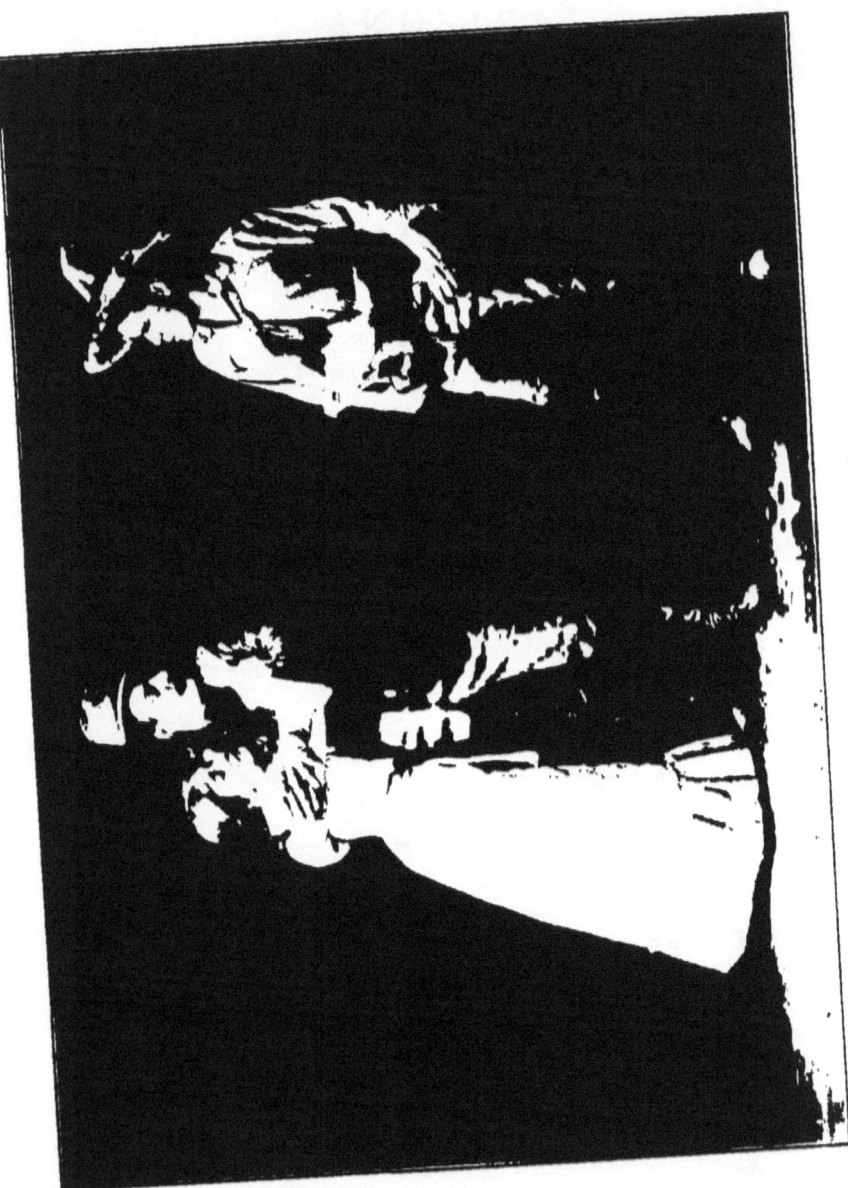

" Who is this man ? "

BONITA.

No—none—[*She takes the side comb from her hair and regards it.*] none—definite.

HODGMAN.

[*With some earnestness.*] Do you know—you—you 've never seemed like an Arizona girl to me—Miss—Bonita?
[*The glow of the sunset fades into the pale blue of moonlight.*

BONITA.

Oh ! well, I went to school in 'Frisco.

HODGMAN.

Nor like a California one, either.

BONITA.

Haven't I?
[ESTRELLA *comes from the house and pauses, overhearing.*

HODGMAN.

[*Quite earnestly.*] God's country is down East, just between the Mohawk River and Long Island.

BONITA.

You call that—God's country, do you?

HODGMAN.

Yes, and it 's where God's loveliest creatures seem to belong. If you were to spend one Autumn there, you 'd be heart-broken over every one you 've wasted on these ashes. *You* seem to belong there, little girl.

ESTRELLA.

[*In fateful monotone.*] Oh—Bonita.

BONITA.

Yes? [HODGMAN *crosses with slight show of annoyance.*

ESTRELLA.

[*In lighter manner.*] Why aren't you dressing?

BONITA.

I *am* late. Excuse me, Captain.

[HODGMAN *bows.* BONITA *goes into the house.*

ESTRELLA.

Captain——

HODGMAN.

Yes?

ESTRELLA.

Of course, Bonita *is* one of God's loveliest creatures, but [*Pause*] if I were you, I 'd let some one else tell her so.

HODGMAN.

There was nothing in that, was there?

ESTRELLA.

Something that, for the moment, made me wonder if you were not the most insincere man I ever met.

HODGMAN.

Why!—why the young lady is your sister.

ESTRELLA.

That is what *I* urge. You can't use it in your *defense.*

HODGMAN.

Is defense needed?

ESTRELLA.

You were trying to *impress* Bonita.

HODGMAN.

Yes? [*Pause.*] And your look is saying that I had also tried to impress *you*.

ESTRELLA.

[*Rebukingly.*] I am the wife of—your Colonel, Captain Hodgman. You are unpleasantly personal.

HODGMAN.

Certainly not when I spoke to your sister——

ESTRELLA.

You were trying to make Bonita unhappy with her surroundings.

HODGMAN.

The law of progress——

ESTRELLA.

You have taken the content from my life for your amusement. Let her's alone.

HODGMAN.

Amusement, Estrella! [*Pause.*] Look at me—— [*Estrella looks at him and then looks away.*] I didn't say glance at me. Look!

ESTRELLA.

[*Looking at him.*] Why! I hope you don't think I fear you, Captain.

HODGMAN.

[*Smiling.*] Fear me—of course not. [*Pause.*] Now, don't say I stole your peace of mind. Lethargy isn't content. You were dreaming here in the hot sands like a torpid nestling. I talked of the ocean and the smell of the low tide, and you began to wake up—you breathed deeper—[*Pause and a slight movement *of his hand before her face.*]—as you are breathing now.   [*Smiles and watches her.*]   The languor went out of your eyes, [*Pause*] as it is going now, and your soul came into them——

E S T R E L L A.

I have the love of the best man in the world.

H O D G M A N.

Which should *fill* every empty hour, and yet——

E S T R E L L A.

And I love *him*.

H O D G M A N.

Almost like a father.   [*Laughs and turns from her.*

E S T R E L L A.

[*Pause.*]   You 're not a man.   You 're a devil.

H O D G M A N.

[*Again catching her gaze.*]   No! This is the wilderness, and all these things I show you, but I don't ask you to bow down and worship me.   *I 'm* the idolator.

E S T R E L L A.

I don't want your interest.

H O D G M A N.

I love you—love you—as I 'd love a rose—to look at—to in-hale—to hold.

E S T R E L L A.

Or—perhaps—to crush.

HODGMAN.

If it were sweeter so—to crush ! [*Pause; he looks at her with fierce ardor, as awaiting some reply; she returns his look, and after a moment gives him her hand.*] Estrella !

ESTRELLA.

[*After a look to right.*] Leonard ! [HODGMAN *starts to embrace her; she shrinks back; he retains her hand, stoops and kisses it;* DENTON *enters through gate;* ESTRELLA *quickly withdraws hand;* HODGMAN *glances at her in surprise, and from the direction of her gaze apprehends* DENTON. *He turns.*

DENTON.

[*Saluting.*] Captain.

HODGMAN.

Mr. Denton.

DENTON.

That horse of Shannon's—unfit for saddle to-morrow.

HODGMAN.

Will he do with a blanket ?

DENTON.

Yes, sir.

HODGMAN.

Very well.

[HODGMAN *follows* ESTRELLA, *who has gone toward dining-room. He again notes her steady regard of* DENTON, *who has not moved, and turns sharply upon him.*] Anything further, Mr. Denton ?

DENTON.

[*In defiant undertone.*] Only supper, I believe, sir.

ESTRELLA.

Come, Captain. [*She touches his arm and goes.* HODGMAN *follows her to door;* DENTON *comes to the table;* HODGMAN *turns and meets* DENTON'S *gaze; is about to exclaim upon him when* ESTRELLA *again touches his arm. A burst of laughter is heard in the dining-room in response to some joke of* CANBY'S.] Captain; Come!
[HODGMAN *follows* ESTRELLA *into the dining-room.* DENTON *stands looking after them.*

CURTAIN

THE SECOND ACT

HE scene represents the interior of the drawing-room of COLONEL BONHOM'S *quarters at Fort Grant, Arizona. The wall to the left of the stage is occupied by a large open fireplace, with inglenook seats on either side of it, and facing each other. A moose head is over the mantel shelf. Below the fireplace, that is, nearer the audience, is a big wooden settle, with its back to the wall. The settle is furnished with sofa pillows and fitted with a shelf overhead. The wall space above the fireplace is filled by a piano. The wall facing the audience obliques slightly to the right, so that the right wall is a third shorter than the left. The back wall is occupied by a single door to the left of the center and by a large window filling its remaining space. The door opens into a hall. The window lets upon the parade ground. A smaller window adjoins this in the left wall. All of the openings in the wall show the regular adobe thickness of three feet, making in the windows recesses deep enough for chairs. The walls are stained a deep terra cotta. The ceiling is of sage green, ribbed by the natural wood of the beams. The settle and mantel are sage green. Some framed engravings are hung upon the walls. The furniture of the room is simple and old-fashioned. The windows are fitted with green blinds against the sash and with sage green portieres flush with the walls. In a jog of the left wall, near the auditor, is a Mexican loom.*

The time is midnight. Outside is the light of the moon. Indoors are a couple of hanging-lamps and the light from the fireplace. A few empty dishes, rumpled napkins and some spoons indicate the recent serving of refreshments. The music of a military band playing a valse is heard outside.

DOCTOR FENLON is seated at the fireplace smoking a cigarette. MISS MACCULLAGH, the school teacher, stands beside him in an evening gown. Her eyes snap and she taps impatiently with her toe.

MISS MACCULLAGH.
Why don't you smoke out-of-doors?

DOCTOR.
I do.

MISS MACCULLAGH
Are you ever serious, Doctor Fenlon?

DOCTOR.
Do you mean in my intentions?

MISS MACCULLAGH.
I mean in your life. I don't believe you ever had a genuine sorrow.

DOCTOR.
[*Taking the cigarette from his mouth.*] Huh! Laid down three queens last night with nothing against 'em but a pair of ten spots.

MISS MACCULLAGH.

[*Showing anger, as school teachers sometimes do.*] God gave you brains, Doctor Fenlon. He put your ears far enough back to leave room for some perception.

DOCTOR.

[*Apologetically.*] Can't see through a pasteboard.

MISS MACCULLAGH.

And yet you dawdle your life away over a pack of cards.

DOCTOR.

Can't make 'em take medicine when they ain't sick—that is, not always.

MISS MACCULLAGH.

Why not write? Why not read? Why not walk? Why, you aren't even in good physical condition.

DOCTOR.

[*Placidly.*] Oh—you're jealous. [MISS MACCULLAGH *goes out angrily.*]

[SERGEANT KELLAR *enters briskly from the left of the door, followed by his daughter* LENA. LENA *carries a tray.*

KELLAR.

Clean everything here, first, den de porch. [*Picks up a spoon.*] Here is a spoon on de floor, somebody step on him. [*Straightens spoon, throws it in dish, and goes out.* LENA *goes about collecting plates.*

LENA.

Can I have your plate, Doctor?

DOCTOR.

Yes. [LENA *takes* DOCTOR's *plate, and starts out.*] LENA!

LENA.

[*Pausing in the doorway.*] Doctor?

DOCTOR.

That man doing anything for you?

LENA.

[*With furtive look to the outside.*] I won't let him do any-thing for me.

DOCTOR.

[*Rising and speaking in reassuring tone.*] But you must. It is n't only of yourself you have to think. Now let me *speak* to him, and make some arrangement for the support of that little one.

LENA.

My father—I am afraid he will find out. My father would kill him.

DOCTOR.

But your father won't find out.

LENA.

You would n't tell my *father* who it was?

DOCTOR.

No.

LENA.

You have n't told anybody?

DOCTOR.

No.

LENA.

Because you are the only one I have told his name.

KELLAR.

[*Re-appearing busily.*] Come, Lena, make quick.

LENA.

Yes, Father. [*She goes out looking back appealingly to the* Doctor.

DOCTOR.

Must compliment you, Sergeant, on your part of the entertainment.

KELLAR.

[*Tentatively.*]   Yes.   [*The music outside ceases.*

DOCTOR.

Could n't have been smoother at Delmonico's.

KELLAR.

[*With ill-concealed pride.*]   I have worked at a restaurant in Berlin.

DOCTOR.

Lena is very handy, too.

KELLAR.

[*His brow clouding.*]   Lena would be a good waitress, but it is better she is a striker for Miss Canby.

DOCTOR.

Much better.

KELLAR.

Dat Canby's ranch is a nice place for a girl, better dan a dam't Cavalry Post.

[Bonita *appears at the window with* Miss MacCullagh.

BONITA.

Sergeant !   Have you seen Mr. Denton ?

SERGEANT.

Not now.   Lieutenant is officer of the day.

    [MISS MACCULLAGH *re-enters and joins the* DOCTOR *by
the fireside.*

BONITA.

I know. [*Then complainingly to the* DOCTOR.] But he had that
last dance with me.

MISS MACCULLAGH.

Why don't you dance, Doctor?   [BONITA *leaves the window
and appears in the doorway.*]   You could, I believe, if you wore
suspenders.   [DOCTOR *hitches up his trousers.* BONITA *enters.*

SERGEANT.

[*To* BONITA.]   Ven are you going to de ranch back again,
Miss Canby?

    [MISS MACCULLAGH *is talking animatedly to the* DOCTOR,
who listens tolerantly.

BONITA.

As soon as Colonel gets home from this trip of to-night.

KELLAR.

You must oxgooze, but you take Lena?   Yez?

BONITA.

Take Lena?   Yes, indeed, I couldn't do without Lena.

KELLAR.

Good!   Much oblige.

    [DENTON *appears in doorway.* *He wears his side arms,
indicating that he is on duty.*

DENTON.

Forgive me, Miss Canby, but I couldn't make it. Sergeant.

KELLAR.

'Tenant.

DENTON.

Report to Col. Bonham that the ambulance is ready. [*Comes to chair down to the right where* BONITA *sits.*

KELLAR.

Yes, sir. [*He goes out the door and to the right.*

MISS MACCULLAGH.

You know, Dr. Fenlon, your—your indifference to dress is a thing of comment in the Post ?

DOCTOR.

Well, that 's a God's blessing these dull times, isn't it ?
[*He chuckles to himself.* MISS MCCULLAGH *leaves him and goes to the doorway.*

MISS MACCULLAGH.

How does he expect any woman to take an interest in him ?
[*She goes out, passes the big window and disappears.*

DOCTOR.

[*Following.*] Don't go 'way mad. [*He pauses at door.*]
Pardon, Miss Canby, but understood smoking was permitted in this room.

BONITA.

Everywhere. [DOCTOR *follows* MISS MACCULLAGH.] I believe you didn't care to dance with me. [*She crosses in mock dignity to the fireplace.*

DENTON.

[*Following her.*] You know better. You know 'way down in your wild Arizona heart that I 'd almost mutiny to be with you, don't you?

BONITA.

Why, you don't even keep your appointments.

[*Music is resumed outside.*

DENTON.

The Colonel 's going to Los Angeles, and I 've had to make ready for him. But I 'll stand under your window to-night, and I 'll spend every hour at your side to-morrow.

BONITA.

I 'm going to sleep to-morrow.

DENTON.

Lucky girl to be able. I 've almost forgotten how.

BONITA.

Forgotten how to sleep?

DENTON.

Yes—I 'm worse than no soldier at all. There 's a girl's name sings in my ears, and I don't hear the bugle. Captain 's sent me to headquarters twice in a week, and I have to take it; because what would be a Colonel's answer if a man with one bar on his shoulder said, " I forgot parade, sir, because I was dreaming of your wife's sister !"

BONITA.

[*Laughing.*] He 'd probably answer that you hadn't forgotten to sleep.

"Every Lieutenant talks that way, Mr. Denton."

DENTON.

Day dreams—Bonita—day dreams—night and day. Believe me ?

BONITA.

I think that's something you learn at West Point. Every Lieutenant talks that way, Mr. Denton. [*She recrosses to the chair at right.*

DENTON.

To you ?

BONITA.

To all girls.

DENTON.

Miss Canby.

BONITA.

Of course. Did you ever see a girl near an army Post that did n't have a gown trimmed with soldiers' buttons ? [*She sits.*

DENTON.

[*Bending over her.*] But what of that ?

BONITA.

Every button a vow.

DENTON.

[*Ardently.*] If each vow of mine for *you* took a button, I 'd have to report in pajamas.

[HODGMAN *and* ESTRELLA *pass the window and come in through the door.*

HODGMAN.

Oh! Mr. Denton, anything wanted ?

DENTON.

Reporting to Colonel Bonham, sir.

HODGMAN.

Oh!   [*He joins* ESTRELLA *at the settle.*

BONITA.

[*Noticing* HODGMAN's *manner and rising sympathetically.*] Have
I made trouble for you ?

DENTON.

[*As she looks at* HODGMAN.]   Not there.   Here.   [*Hand on
heart.* BONITA *puts fan on his lips.* DENTON *takes hold of it.*]
Where are those side combs ?   [*They go to the window.*

ESTRELLA.

[*With* HODGMAN.] Don't talk about it, Leonard, until the
Colonel has gone, or I shall scream.

HODGMAN.

But Estrella, dear, only to ask if you followed instructions. Is
everything ready ?

ESTRELLA.

Yes, everything.

HODGMAN.

Good !   Now, keep your nerve.   In fifty-six hours we 'll be
in New Orleans, and then—   [*Music outside ceases.*

ESTRELLA.

Careful—careful— .
                [COLONEL *enters with* MISS MACCULLAGH *on his arm.*

COLONEL.

[*Laughing.*]   Estrella—

ESTRELLA.

Yes, dear.

COLONEL.

Miss MacCullagh hasn't decided—

MISS MACCULLAGH.

[*Trying to stop him.*]   Now, Colonel.

ESTRELLA.

What is it, Miss MacCullagh?

COLONEL.

[*Laughing and holding her hands.*]   Has n't picked out an officer.   Now, I say, a girl that can't find a fellow in the Eleventh, doesn't deserve one.   Even offered a Captain. [ESTRELLA *and* CAPTAIN *exchange glances.*

MISS MACCULLAGH.

'Tisn't fair, is it?

> [*She goes to* BONITA—LIEUTENANT HALLOCK *and* YOUNG *enter and join the young people at the window.*

DENTON.

[*Saluting.*]   Colonel.

COLONEL.

Mr. Denton.

DENTON.

Ambulance is ready.

COLONEL.

I know.   Thank you.   See here, Mr. Denton, why haven't you been dancing?

DENTON.

Duty, sir; officer of the day.

COLONEL.

Oh. [*Pause.* DENTON *joins* BONITA *a moment, then goes into the doorway.*] Well, dear. [*To* ESTRELLA.] Ambulance is here. I'm going to be excused. You young folks 'll have to get along without me.

DENTON.

Ambulance here, Colonel, or at headquarters ?

COLONEL.

Here.

DENTON.

Yes sir. [*Salutes.*] Ladies. [*He bows and goes out.*

COLONEL.

[*At door and looking after* DENTON.] Mr. Hallock.

HALLOCK.

Colonel.

COLONEL.

What 's the matter with Harry ?

HALLOCK.

Oh, nothing serious, I think, sir.

COLONEL.

[*Coming back.*] I want you juniors to understand that I haven't any favorite officer. Even my adjutant 's a matter of business. But, Bonita, I have a favorite protege. That boy's father and I in the Washita Campaign made a ride with papers from Custer to Miles, that you 'll find in the printed records of the War department. Finished by trotting – bang—into Miles's dining-room, on the same horse. Denton insensible—me, crazy. Papers in Denton's water-soaked boot—cut it off— [*Pause.* DOCTOR *re-enters.*] And right now, I 'd be willing to—Well, just understand, I like his boy. [*Pause.*] Now, what 's the matter with him? Come, I see you know something, Doctor.

Doctor.
Don't believe it 's in my department, Colonel.

Colonel.
But, what is it?

Miss MacCullagh.
Poker! It 's that dreadful game you permit at the Officers' Club.

Colonel.
Poker?—'m—I had n't noticed Harry losing much.

Doctor.
Only a few hundred, I believe, but—

Colonel.
[*Astonished.*] A few hundred? Gad! [*Pause.*

Doctor.
I don't think it 's the money, Colonel. Denton isn't like the rest of us.

Colonel.
I should say not, if he doesn't mind the money.

Doctor.
He doesn't like merely vegetating. I really think Denton 'd be happier in some large business, where his activity could be engaged. He says a man rusts out in the army.

COLONEL.

Gad! If somebody in Washington had a little backbone, we wouldn't be rusting. [*He goes to the door and turns.*] Well, come, little gal, I 'll change my duds.

ESTRELLA.

Excuse me. [*She and* COLONEL *disappear left.*

HODGMAN.

Guess it 's about time for us all to go.

DOCTOR.

Yes, nearly. [MISS MACCULLAGH *goes out with* MR. YOUNG.

HALLOCK.

[*Offering arm to* BONITA.] I might have a minute's promenade.

BONITA.

Yes, and tell me something about Mr. Denton's losses. [*She goes out with* HALLOCK.

DOCTOR.

A few hundred covers it, Captain, does n't it?

HODGMAN.

Covers what? [*Walking slowly toward door.*

DOCTOR.

Denton's losings.

HODGMAN.

[*Easily.*] How should I know.

DOCTOR.

Oh! then he 's paid, has he? Thought you had a record. Don't go.

HODGMAN.

[*Lightly.*]   Think I will.   Getting late.

DOCTOR.

But I want a word with you.

HODGMAN.

[*At door.*]   Poker sermon ?

DOCTOR.

[*After lighting cigarette.*]   Woman.

HODGMAN.

[*Quickly alert.*]   Woman ?   [*The* DOCTOR *nods.*]   What woman ?

DOCTOR.

Lena.

HODGMAN.

Lena ?   Lena who ?

DOCTOR.

Sergeant Kellar's daughter.

HODGMAN.

What about her ?

DOCTOR.

Professional secret, but I have her permission to speak.   [*Pause.*] She says your secret, too.

HODGMAN.

I don't know what you mean.

DOCTOR.

[*Smiling.*]   And you 're a cavalryman.   [*Pause.*]   Well, Captain, there 's a little guest at the Catholic Nursery in El Paso. I told them his board would be paid.

HODGMAN.

Oh—I suppose we all contribute ?

DOCTOR.

[*Rising angrily.*]   That's very nasty, Hodgman, but you'll have to put up just the same.   [*He crosses to the fireplace.*

HODGMAN.

Rot !

DOCTOR.

Kellar holds the sharp-shooter's medal for the regiment. [KELLAR *enters and goes to window, closing it.*]   Just speaking of you, Sergeant.   Closing up ?

KELLAR.

Only this side, sir.   Dance is over.   Colonel goes away besides.

DOCTOR.

[*Watching* HODGMAN.]   Yes ?   Er—a—Sergeant, are you as good with a six-shooter as you are with the carbine.

KELLAR.

No, sir.   Two men better dan me wid six-shooters.

DOCTOR.

[*Smiling.*]   Oh! Only two, eh ?

KELLAR.

Yezza.   'Tenant Denton and Private Kane, B Troop.
     [LENA *appears in the door.*

HODGMAN.

You can go to hell, Fenlon.   [*He turns on his heel and goes quickly out.*

LENA.

[*Apprehensively.*] Doctor.

DOCTOR.

[*Following* HODGMAN.] Will you put that permission in writing, Captain. [*He disappears.*

KELLAR.

[*Starting after them.*] Ha! They can't fight at the Colonel's dance.

LENA.

Father!

KELLAR.

[*Turning in the doorway.*] What's the matter, Lena? [*He again turns away.*

LENA.

Father—

KELLAR.

[*Impatiently.*] Yes—yes—yes.

LENA.

I have found a letter.

KELLAR.

Found a letter? [*Comes back into the room.*

LENA.

From the Captain.

KELLAR.

His letter?

LENA.

To Missus. I saw him hand it to her. After a while *I* got it.

KELLAR.

Well, Lena, that is not your business. What everybody talks in the Post—you do not hear. If an old man like the Colonel marries his granddaughter—let 'em talk—let 'em talk. I have this told you before.

LENA.

But they are going.

KELLAR.

Who ?

LENA.

The Colonel's wife.

KELLAR.

[*Shaking his head.*]   Only the Colonel.

LENA.

But afterwards—with the Captain.   I know.

KELLAR.

Sh! [*Pause. In lowered tone.*]   Well, we must pretend not to know.   And, when they come back, still not to know— nothing.

LENA.

But not to come back.

KELLAR.

Not come back ?

LENA.

He is going—that is it—forever.

KELLAR.

You talk foolishness.   Forever ?   Leave a Captain's pay ?

LENA.

She is rich.   Every jewel is packed up.   Believe me, father. I know.   [*Produces letter.*]   And his letter——[*As she gives the letter to* KELLAR, *voices are heard in the hall.*

KELLAR.

Sh!

[*The* COLONEL *and* ESTRELLA *enter.* *The* COLONEL *has his cap and cape.*

COLONEL.

Sergeant, have my bag put in the ambulance.

SERGEANT.

It is in the hall.

ESTRELLA.

In my room, the big bag. Lena knows. [KELLAR *and* LENA *go.*] Frank, dear, be careful, won't you?

COLONEL.

[*Laughing and chucking her chin.*] Why, little gal, what's the matter to-night? Careful? Pulman car, fine hotel, and I, an old campaigner, who needs only a blanket.

[*Again the music begins outside.*

ESTRELLA.

Yes, and that makes you careless. I don't want anything to happen to you. I want you to live for years and years, and forget what a foolish girl you married.

COLONEL.

Foolish girl, indeed! Here, none o' that. Why, little one, you mustn't get the idea, because I don't dance, that I think dancing's foolish. Gad! I 've danced all night and ridden both days to do it. Why, Strella, you never take a step or laugh a note, that your silly old martinet of a husband doesn't skip and laugh with you—in his heart—but, jingo! after sixty, you can't

two-step this outline of mine around, except by platoon.
Ha, ha!

E S T R E L L A.

'T isn't that, but when you 're away and you think about
me, I want you to know that I respected you more than anybody
in the world, and that I think you 're noble and good—

C O L O N E L.

[*Burlesquely.*]   Help—help!   Officer of the guard!

E S T R E L L A.

And—and—any mistakes I make, are because I 've been
spoiled, and always had my own way—and—

C O L O N E L.

Ha, Ha! [*Stops her with loud laughter and kisses her;* DENTON
appears in doorway.

D E N T O N.

Pardon, Colonel, but had to put mules to the ambulance. That
West bound train goes through at three thirty, and two hours and
a half isn't any too much time for twenty miles.

C O L O N E L.

Right.   [*Kisses* ESTRELLA *again.*]   Good-bye.   [*He goes out,
followed by* ESTRELLA.

C O L O N E L.

[*Outside.*]   Good-bye, Bonita.   Make it a wing shot, if you
want to kiss me.

[DENTON *follows to door;* KELLAR *enters.*

K E L L A R.

Lieutenant—'Tenant Denton.   One minute, please. [*They
come down together.*

DENTON.

Well, Sergeant ?

KELLAR.

[*Handing letter.*]   My Lena—found this letter.   She thinks they mean to go to-night.   [DENTON *reads, with an increasing frown.*]   Missus Bonham's horse is saddled.   Lena says, things packed to travel.

DENTON.

There is no address or name.

KELLAR.

Lena saw Captain Hodgman give it to Mrs. Bonham.

DENTON.

[*Still reading.*]   God Almighty!

KELLAR.

'Tenant.   [DENTON *looks up.*]   Lena says, a roll of diamonds in a buckskin, big as my wrist.

DENTON.

[*In disgust.*]   Ha!   [*Pause.*]   Don't speak of this, Sergeant.
    [BONITA *enters.*

BONITA.

Well, the Colonel 's gone, and it seems like the fun had all gone with him.

DENTON.

A good deal of it has.   [*Puts the letter in his breast and crosses moodily to the settle.*

KELLAR.

Orders, sir ?   [*A* SERGEANT-MAJOR *appears in the doorway.*

DENTON.

That's all.

SERGEANT-MAJOR.

Sergeant Kellar.   Sergeant of the Guard sick.   You'll have to take his place.

KELLAR.

All right.   [*The* SERGEANT-MAJOR *disappears.*]   Oh! it's a dog's life, in the army.   [KELLAR *goes out.*

BONITA.

[*Regarding* DENTON.]   Is this Officer-of-the-day business such a depressing thing?

DENTON.

Pardon me.   A trifle pre-occupied.   Oh no, rather a matter of form in peace times, this "Officer-of-the-day business."   The Colonel goes in heavily for discipline, however, and I think he likes us to closely observe the regulations.

BONITA.

He likes you.

DENTON.

I'm sure of that.   Perhaps you know that he got me my appointment to the Academy?   [*He crosses to where she stands at right.*

BONITA.

Did he?

DENTON.

[*With emotion.*]   Been kind of a father to me, always.   I couldn't begin to tell you all that Colonel Bonham has done for me, and mine.

[HODGMAN *in civilian dress comes quickly into the room.*

BONITA.

Why, Captain, in citizen's dress?

HODGMAN.

Yes. I thought I'd ride as far as the village with the Colonel, but changed my mind.

DENTON.

[*Sullenly.*] Couldn't one do that in uniform?

HODGMAN.

Mr. Denton!

DENTON.

[*Saluting.*] Captain.

HODGMAN.

Send word to that band-master to turn in. Get the Post quiet.

DENTON.

Yes, sir. [*He salutes and goes.*

BONITA.

Take me with you, Mr. Denton. [*She runs after* DENTON *in comic affectation of terror.*

HODGMAN.

[*At the mantel.*] By God, what a finish! But, after twenty years in the beastly service, with its favoritism and political promotions, the lick-spittal 's sent to the sea shore, and I in this sage-brush and alkali. [*Looks about.*] And now, this Dutch girl with more trouble for me.

[ESTRELLA *appears in the doorway.*

ESTRELLA.

Leonard.

HODGMAN.

Estrella.

ESTRELLA.

Alone ?

HODGMAN.

Alone. *[The band outside stops playing.*

ESTRELLA.

It 's awful, isn't it ? *[She comes down right and sits.*

HODGMAN.

What ?

ESTRELLA.

To go.

HODGMAN.

Awful, if you think it awful. To me it 's life.

ESTRELLA.

He doesn't dream of it—and he 's been so good to me. Oh! if I 'd never known you, Leonard.

HODGMAN.

But you do know me, and you knew me as soon as you knew him, but he had an eagle on his shoulder ; and youth and love and devotion couldn't count against an epaulette.

ESTRELLA.

Haven't they counted, Leonard—haven't they. Am I not giving my immortal soul for them ?

HODGMAN.

[Bending over her.] Forgive me.
[BONITA returns.

BONITA.

They 're all gone, Estrella.

[HODGMAN *goes to the settle.*

ESTRELLA.

[*Rising.*]   Yes, dear—it 's been a long, gay evening for you.

BONITA.

What 's the matter, Estrella ?

ESTRELLA.

Tired a little, dear.   Come, say good night to the Captain and go to your room.

BONITA.

[*Laughing.*]   Like a good little girl!   [*To* HODGMAN.]   I suppose, if I get to be a hundred, I shall always be " little sister " to Estrella.   Well, good night, Captain.   [*Offering her hand.*

HODGMAN.

[*Shaking her hand.*]   Good night.   I congratulate you on your evening.

BONITA.

Wasn't it gorgeous ?

ESTRELLA.

Good night, dear.   [*Kisses* BONITA.

BONITA.

Good night.   [*She holds* ESTRELLA's *hand.*]   I say, Estrella, of course, you 're the chaperone, but if it 's so late that I 've got to go to bed, isn't it a shade late for married chaperones, and captains with black mustaches ?

ESTRELLA.

Sh! Bonita, you don't know what you are saying. Captain's
in command of the Post now, and there are important subjects to
discuss.

BONITA.

Ow! Excuse me.

> [*She walks quickly and stiffly to the door, turns and
> salutes, and runs out laughing heartily.* ESTRELLA
> *looks at the* CAPTAIN *and falls into the chair weeping.*

HODGMAN.

[*After closing the door.*]   We won't get very far, Estrella, on
that kind of mettle.

ESTRELLA.

Is it best to go now ?   Is this the time ?

HODGMAN.

The only time.   This trip of the Colonel's to Los Angeles ; a
conference of this department.

ESTRELLA.

Well ?

HODGMAN.

Getting ready!   The talk is about over.   We may be ordered
to the front any day, and then—

ESTRELLA.

There might be glory for you.

HODGMAN.

[*Moodily.*]   I have a feeling that I should never come back.
Officers are shining marks.   You and I would meet no more.
[*Pause.*]   But if you haven't the courage—

ESTRELLA.

[*Stoutly.*] There! [*Rises.*] I'm as brave as you are now.

HODGMAN.

Good! Then get ready to ride.

ESTRELLA.

I have only my gown to change.

HODGMAN.

[*With averted gaze.*] And your—personal effects—the—the jewels—

ESTRELLA.

[*Smiling bitterly.*] Here. [*She takes a package from her breast.*

HODGMAN.

Don't resent my remembering them, because they're all we shall have with which to travel. Besides, you ordered them, remember.

ESTRELLA.

Of course, Leonard. Forgive my smile. But I resent anything that seems to take your first thought from me. [*She extends the package toward him.*] Take them.

HODGMAN.

[*Walking away.*] No, let's call it off, Estrella, if we are to be reminded that yours is the money.

ESTRELLA.

Nonsense, Leonard. [*She follows.*

HODGMAN.

And yet, at the first necessity, you smile.

ESTRELLA.

I explain that, and say forgive me.   [*She again offers the
jewels.*

HODGMAN.

Oh, well—[*He takes them with a show of reluctance.*

ESTRELLA.

Now, don't pout, Leonard, or I shall break down.

HODGMAN.

I won't then.   Come.   [*He takes her hand.*]   I 'll make
haste with my own horse, and look after yours.   There—hurry
now, yourself.   [*They go to the door,* HODGMAN *opens it disclosing*
DENTON *in doorway;* HODGMAN *slightly starts back;* ESTRELLA
gives a little cry of alarm.

HODGMAN.

Well, Mr. Denton.

DENTON.

An order came to C troop stables to saddle your horse.

HODGMAN.

Well ?

DENTON.

I countermanded the order.

HODGMAN.

The order was mine.

DENTON.

I countermanded it.

HODGMAN.

Yes ?

DENTON.

Yes.

HODGMAN.

By what authority.

DENTON.

Officer of the day.

HODGMAN.

I am your Captain.

DENTON.

Still, the horse won't be taken from the stables.

HODGMAN.

This is insubordination.

DENTON.

It is more, sir, if you persist.

HODGMAN.

What do you mean?

DENTON.

I mean death. [*His hand goes to his holster.*

ESTRELLA.

Death! Leonard!

HODGMAN.

Mr. Denton, you are using threatening language to your commanding officer, and you have your hand upon your holster.

DENTON.

Holster, yes—drawn, if you will. [*He draws his revolver.*

ESTRELLA.

Lieutenant Denton! You are in your Colonel's house.

DENTON.

[*Speaking to* ESTRELLA *but watching* HODGMAN.] I'm glad

you remember it, Madam. I am in my Colonel's house, so is this man. I have here his letter, arranging this departure, and if he tries it, I am here to kill him.

ESTRELLA.

No—no! Oh, Denton, don't—don't make a row. Think of the scandal. Think—think of Bonita!

DENTON.

[*In a fateful undertone.*] I am thinking of Bonita, but most, I think of that brave old soldier to whom I owe almost my existence—to whom, as Colonel of my regiment, I owe allegiance; and I swear to God, Hodgman, if you attempt this wrong upon him, I 'll just kill you.

HODGMAN.

[*Pause.*] You 've got the drop on me, Denton, and I think you 're fool enough to shoot. [*Pause.*] As this lady's name is involved, I 've got to do what you say.

DENTON.

Then, go. [*He steps aside, leaving the doorway free.*

HODGMAN.

Where ? To my quarters ?

DENTON.

To hell, if you care to, as you told the Doctor. [HODGMAN *starts at mention of the* DOCTOR'S *name. The men exchange glances.* HODGMAN *takes a step toward the door, and* DENTON *again interposes.*] But, wait! [*Pause.* DENTON *looks from one to the other.*] There are some jewels, wrapped in a piece of chamois skin ; I 'll take those. [*Pause.* DENTON *extends his*

hand toward HODGMAN. HODGMAN *hands him the packet.*]   I was
as sure he had them as I was that he 'd ordered the horses.   Your
money, that 's all.

ESTRELLA.

The world ought to pity a woman who has money.

HODGMAN.

You 're devilish careful to have your gun when you make this
play, ain't you, Denton ?

DENTON.

[*Replacing revolver in its holster.*]   A blackguard always ;
nearly expelled from the Corps Cadets ; mixed up nastily, after
that, in the Leavenworth papers ; and even now there 's a woman
in this very Post with a greater claim on him than yours.

HODGMAN.

You pup !

ESTRELLA.

Whom do you mean ?

DENTON.

I mean that poor little girl of Kellar's.

ESTRELLA.

[*Turning away sick at heart.*]   Oh!

HODGMAN.

Mrs. Bonham, I swear to you—

ESTRELLA.

No—no!   I feel that it is true.   Oh!   [*She breaks into sobs
and leans on the mantel.*

HODGMAN.

Look at me.

DENTON.

[*Interposing.*] She won't look at you, but I will. [*Pause.*]
Now go !

HODGMAN.

[*Stopping in the doorway.*] If Kellar's daughter told *all* she
knows, Mrs. Bonham, this gentleman might not stand so highly
with Bonita.
      [DENTON *puts his hand over* HODGMAN's *mouth.*

DENTON.

That lady's name is not for your lips.

HODGMAN.

[*Pausing and with defiance.*] It 's to a finish, you—beauty.
                [*Goes out and* DENTON *closes the door.*

DENTON.

[*Pause.*] And now, Mrs. Bonham, I want your parole. [He
goes to mantel.

ESTRELLA.

Oh, Mr. Denton, you don't understand. You don't know
how desperate a woman may become ; and—it sounds empty
and foolish as an excuse to say that—a thing like this has grown
—grown so gradually that the woman, herself, can't quite understand it—and yet—[*Pause, followed by impulsive outburst.*]
Yet, it 's as irresistible as any dreadful fate that comes to you
in a dream. The will is paralyzed ; your feet don't step where
you mean they should go. Oh, I can't explain it, and I know I
seem like a willfully wicked woman. [*She sits in the inglenook seat
and covers her face.*

DENTON.

[*Tenderly.*] I think I understand it, Mrs. Bonham. I tried to knock off whisky once, and it was a deuce of a pull. Used to say to myself, " I 'll bet I won't drink this," even while I was pouring it out. Finally got so I 'd bet I hadn't drunk it, after I had. Then one day the Colonel slapped me on the back, and told me to pull up. Stumbled occasionally after that, but he put his arm around me, and now I go in for golf—and tea. [*Pause.*] Most anybody can pull up if the Colonel 's with 'em.

ESTRELLA.

[*Sobbing.*] You 're talking about him just to break my heart.
[*She crosses to the window.*

DENTON.

Yes. [*Pause.*] It ought 'o break your heart, Mrs. Bonham. He 's fifty-two, but he is as young as any of us, and his love for you is the talk of Arizona. He 's as jealous as a Mexican.

ESTRELLA.

I know it.

DENTON.

He 'd take the life of a man, if he thought the man had kissed your hand.

ESTRELLA.

Yes.

DENTON.

You can't beat that for a lover. And now, your parole. Promise me, you 'll never speak to this man again.

ESTRELLA.

Do you think I need to promise ?

DENTON.

Still, your word.

ESTRELLA.

I give it.

DENTON.

Your hand.

ESTRELLA.

You care to take it, Denton ?

DENTON.

Of course. [*As he takes her hand the* COLONEL'S *voice is heard.*

COLONEL.

[*Outside.*] Orderly, fetch in my bag.

ESTRELLA.

The Colonel!   [*She runs to the door and locks it.*

DENTON.

Don't do that !

ESTRELLA.

Hide, Denton, please !   [*She turns to him, appealing.*

DENTON.

Impossible! There is nothing wrong.

ESTRELLA.

But we can't explain. As you said, he 's as jealous as a Spaniard. Go—in the window a moment, and I 'll take him away. Then you can go out. It is you, of whom he has been jealous always. Never Captain Hodgman.

DENTON.

Madness !

COLONEL.

[*Outside.*] Estrella.

ESTRELLA.

Here—here, Colonel. [*Then in a whisper.*] Please, Denton. Give me a chance to retrieve. [DENTON *dumbly expostulates.*

COLONEL.

[*Trying the door.*] Estrella.

ESTRELLA.

Yes, dear, I 'm coming. [*She goes to the door with a last appeal to* DENTON. DENTON *goes into the window.* ESTRELLA *opens the door.* ·

COLONEL.

[*As he enters.*] What 's the matter dear? You 've been crying?

ESTRELLA.

Yes, a little. I came in here and locked the door, because—I—I didn't want Bonita to see me. She 's been so happy to-night. She wasn't in our room, was she?

COLONEL.

No.

ESTRELLA.

Let 's go there, then.

COLONEL.

You—alone in here?

ESTRELLA.

[*Faint-heartedly.*] Yes—alone.

COLONEL.

Where 's Denton.

ESTRELLA.

Denton ?

COLONEL.

Yes. Captain Hodgman 's at the gate. He says he saw Denton come in the house. [ESTRELLA *shakes her head.*] Funny. [*Pause—looks at* ESTRELLA *with growing suspicion.*

ESTRELLA.

Well, let us look.

COLONEL.

I 've been over this floor. [*Pause.*] I wouldn't like Harry to know that we stood doubting him this way, for even a moment. And I won't. [*He goes to the door but again pauses, in suspicion.*] But Hodgman certainly saw somebody. That last batch of recruits had one or two gay birds in it. [*He crosses to the window in the right wall and looks out.*] Hodgman still there.

ESTRELLA.

[*Under her breath.*] My God! [*The* COLONEL *turns and sees* DENTON *behind the curtain of the larger window.*

COLONEL.

What ! [*Pause.*] Mr. Denton ! [DENTON *comes from behind the curtain.* ESTRELLA *appeals to him from behind the* COLONEL. *The men look steadily into each other's eyes.*

COLONEL.

[*After a moment's pause.*] Well, sir ?

DENTON.

I 'd like until to-morrow to explain this—matter—to you.

COLONEL.

Now ! And for God's sake be quick about it. Tell me at once, that I 'm a trusting, old fool, betrayed, as they always are, by the dearest friend. [*He crosses to position between* DENTON *and* ESTRELLA.

DENTON.

No sir—no !

COLONEL.

But the door was locked. [*Pause.*] And she told me she was alone. What other meaning is there to that ?

DENTON.

No other.

COLONEL.

What !

ESTRELLA.

[*Under her breath.*] Denton.

DENTON.

Only that. Mrs. Bonham thought she was alone.

COLONEL.

And you ?

DENTON.

Was there.

COLONEL.

Why ?

DENTON.

Hiding. I heard Mrs. Bonham coming—and—and I hid there.

COLONEL.

Why hide ? Why were you in the house ? [*Pause.*] Not— [*He looks at* ESTRELLA, *then at* DENTON.] There is one other lady here, under my care—a guest of the Eleventh.

DENTON.

[*Quickly and somewhat fiercely.*]   Colonel Bonham!

COLONEL.

Well ?

DENTON.

[*Pause.*]   You—you are also mistaken in that.

COLONEL.

Then why here ?

DENTON.

I 'll answer you to-morrow.

COLONEL.

You 'll answer me now, or I shall place you under guard.

DENTON.

To-morrow.

COLONEL.

Now.   [*Pause. He goes to the door.*]   Sergeant of the guard—
Sergeant.   [*He returns.*]   Will you answer ?   In the name of
the regiment, Denton, don't force me to do this.

[*Pause.   Enter* KELLAR *and the* GUARD, *who come in and
halt at command from* KELLAR.]   Sergeant, take Lieutenant Denton, and confine him under guard in his quarters.

[KELLAR *salutes.* DENTON *gives up his sword and pistol.*
He takes HODGMAN's *letter from his breast in an
attempt at concealment.*

COLONEL.

What is there ?

DENTON.

Nothing, sir.

COLONEL.

Search him.

KELLAR.

[*As* DENTON *demurs.*] I 've got to search you, Lieutenant.

DENTON.

[*In an undertone to* KELLAR.] The letter—for God's sake—that letter.

KELLAR.

Sh ! [*He passes and palms letter.*

COLONEL.

Well ?

KELLAR.

[*With his attention on secreting letter.*] His pipe, I think. No—[*He inadvertently produces the jewels from* DENTON's *breast.*

COLONEL.

What is it ?

KELLAR.

I don't know.

COLONEL.

Open it.

> [KELLAR *opens the jewel roll.* COLONEL *sees contents, takes it, looks at his wife.* DENTON *quickly signals silence.* ESTRELLA *affects astonishment.*

COLONEL.

Sergeant, wait outside.

[KELLAR *goes out with guard.*] Yours, ain't they ?

ESTRELLA.

I think they are—but—

DENTON.

[*Interrupting.*]   Mrs. Bonham—

COLONEL.

[*Turning fiercely upon him.*]   Well, Mr. Denton.

DENTON.

Well, sir.

COLONEL.

How do you come by the possession of these?

DENTON.

[*Pause.*]   I decline to answer.

COLONEL.

You do?

DENTON.

I do.

COLONEL.

Your refusal will leave but one inference.   [*Pause.*]   And, damme, that 's impossible!   Why should an officer of this regiment steal?   [*Pause.*]   Can't you speak?   [*Pause.*]   Mr. Denton.

DENTON.

I 've nothing to say, sir.

COLONEL.

An officer of the Eleventh—[*He breathes heavily.*]   And every one of 'em 's been like a member of my family.   [*Pause.*]   I start out for a journey.   The orderly rushes after me with a telegram, calling it off.   I turn right back, and find—this!   [*Pause and perplexed glance wavering between his wife and the jewels which he holds.*]   I 've been told to-night that you needed money—poker

THE COLONEL

ARIZONA 87

losses—but why not come to me? [*Looks suspiciously at his wife.*] You have either committed a theft, Mr. Denton, or your presence here implies dishonor in this family. [*Regards* ESTRELLA *distrustfully.*

DENTON.

[*Quickly.*] Not that, sir—no.

COLONEL.

[*Turning upon* DENTON *in almost rending anger.*] The thief, then.

ESTRELLA.

He's not a thief. Those trinkets! [DENTON *starts to expostulate.*] I don't care—

COLONEL.

I don't care for them, either. If I owned them, I'd give them all to know that he was completely innocent. [*Pause and a return to* DENTON.] Denton, I knew your father. [*Pause.*] I can't try his boy on so detestable a charge. Don't—don't make me do it. [*The men look at each other for a moment, and the* COLONEL's *tone softens.*] You've been sullen and indifferent lately. You don't like your duty. I'm afraid, my boy, the army isn't the place for you.

DENTON.

[*Slowly apprehending.*] What do you mean, sir?

COLONEL.

I mean you ought to try something else. The only way out of—[*Another waver between the wife and the jewels.*] this thing is for you to resign.

ESTRELLA.

[*Half hysterically.*] No, Colonel, no! [*She throws herself on his breast, sobbing helplessly.*

COLONEL.

[*Looking first at* DENTON, *then down at her with half-closed eyes, that indicate suspicion ; then searchingly at* DENTON *again.*] Your resignation—write it!   [*He points to the writing table.*

> [DENTON *pauses, walks to writing table, turns in dumb appeal to the* COLONEL, *and sits. The* COLONEL *glances a moment at the woman who is sobbing on his shoulder, then, with a look of disgust at the jewels, pushes her roughly from him and dashes the jewels on the floor.*

ESTRELLA.

[*With a step toward* DENTON *and a broken-hearted cry.*]   Oh, Denton!

> [DENTON *rises and turns toward her.*

COLONEL.

[*Turning fiercely upon them.*]   What is it ?   [ESTRELLA *sinks into a chair.* DENTON *sits at table and quickly writes his resignation.*

CURTAIN

THE THIRD ACT

*HE scene represents the interior of the dining-room at* CANBY'S. *There are doors in the walls right and left, and a door and window in the back wall. All these openings show the three-foot thickness common to walls of adobe construction. Through the back door and window appear the court in which the first act took place and the stable beyond it. The walls of this dining-room have been white-washed, but are now a smoky and uneven grey. Two or three prints of game and a powder company's advertising calendar hang about, and there is a profusion of Apache pottery, woven baskets and Indian trophies on shelves over the doors and window. Some Avajo blankets are on the floor for rugs. An olla of drinking water hangs outside the door. To the right is a home-made dresser. In the center is a heavy dowelled table. There are also four or five heavy square dowelled chairs, with seats and backs of cowhide, from which the hair has not been removed.* LENA *is setting the table for luncheon, while* TONY, *the vaquero, sits in the deep adobe window, singing to the accompaniment of his mandolin.*

TONY.

[*Singing.*

Del cielo la estrella Brillante,
El viento que viene del mar,
Sabiendo tu perfidia te adora,
Porque lo llama locura ?

LENA.

That 's a pretty song.

TONY.

I make this song.

LENA.

What does it mean ?

TONY

Major-Domo tell me 'Merican words.

LENA.

Did he ? Well, sing them.

[TONY *sings.*

The heavenly star far above her,
The wind of the infinite sea,
Who know all her perfidy, love her,
Then why call it madness in me ?

LENA.

[*Excitedly.*] Stop.

TONY.

What is the matter ?

LENA.

You sang, " who know all her perfidy.   Are you singing about
me?

TONY.

What is perfidy ?   In Spanish means, " she break my heart."

LENA.

Perfidy is terrible.

TONY.

Is cuss word, like go-damn?

LENA.

[*Regaining self-control.*] No, Tony, I am foolish—it is nothing. [*She sits to the left of the table.*

TONY.

[*Bravely.*] Because, when it is cuss word, I make it. [*Fiercely.*] Go-dam! I love you!

LENA.

Oh! Tony; no—no.

TONY.

[*Quite calm again.*] Yes—yes.

LENA.

[*Tearfully.*] What right have I to be loved by anybody?

TONY.

I go with soldiers. Speaky Spanish. When I come back, you be my wife—Tony Mostano, best vaquero in all the world.

LENA.

When do the soldiers go, Tony?

TONY.

Damn 'f I know.

LENA.

Tony, you mustn't swear so.

TONY.

Oh, well, when I learn 'Merican, I learn good, bad together—

no difference to me.   [TONY *plays " Lieber Augustin" wooingly, with Spanish time, grinning at* LENA.]   Lena, your father is a Dutchman.

LENA.

[*Smiling as she resumes her work.*]   Oh, yes! and that 's a German tune.

TONY.

[*Growing graver and shifting his tune back to the melody of his ballad.*]   When I come back, I build for you a shack.   Not one room, like vaquero shack ; two rooms, with bench on East, where shadow comes.   My mandolin—and damn-to-hell-my-soul, I love you.

LENA.

Tony!

TONY.

You live with me in 'dobe shack ?   You be my wife ?

LENA.

I couldn't, Tony, I couldn't.

TONY.

[*Fiercely.*]   What you want ?   A Dutch fall-off-his-horse Corp'ral ?   I shall stay awake night, forever ?   No! No!

[BONITA *and* MRS. CANBY *come in by the door, left.* TONY *disappears.*]

MRS. CANBY.

[*Catching sight of the fleeing lover.*]   Lena.

LENA.

Yes, ma'am.

MRS. CANBY.

[*Severely.*]   What man was tha* ?

LENA.

Tony.

MRS. CANBY.

Well, the men don't belong in the court, Lena. You must tell them not to come beyond the stables. I wish they'd get their blamed regiment done, and go.

BONITA.

Ma doesn't mean by that, Lena, that if there's any one of them you care to see, he can't come, when your work is done.

LENA.

There is none I care to have come.

[DENTON *appears in the door at back. He is in cowboy attire, with leather " chaps."*

MRS. CANBY.

Is it a round-up?

DENTON.

No, not a herd of any kind. It's the regulars.

BONITA.

[*Brightly.*] The Eleventh?

DENTON.

I think so. What's the matter with Tony? [BONITA *turns and looks at* LENA.] Oh! [*Pause and smile.*] What is it, Lena?

LENA.

He was playing his mandolin——[*She stops in embarrassment and runs out of the door, right.*

DENTON.

She might do worse than Tony. He wants to quit again, and I'd rather lose most any man from the company than Tony.

MRS. CANBY.

I 'll see him myself. I promised Estrella I 'd look after Lena ; and if Tony 's in earnest she 'll have to marry him. [*She disappears into the court after* TONY.

BONITA.

You say the Eleventh is coming, Major-Domo ?

DENTON.

Yes, ordered to the Gulf, I believe. [*He lays his hat and gauntlets on the window-sill.*

BONITA.

Then they won't need the volunteers, will they ? [*She sits at right of table.*

DENTON.

Yes, miss. [*He comes down beside her.*

BONITA.

But why do *you* go ? Pa needs you here. He says you 're the best Major-Domo the ranch ever had.

DENTON.

[*Sadly.*] But I 'm not a cattle-man at heart, Miss Canby. When I quit the service, I wasn't needed. But, with war in sight, and the President calling for men, a chap that 's had his bread and butter, and everything he knows in the world, given him by his country, can't hang back. [*He goes behind the table and to the left.*

BONITA.

You 're only one.

DENTON.

Yes, but the only one among these cowboys with the knowledge that can help them. It 's no use, Miss. The boys like me. They 've 'lected me Captain of a company, and I 've got to go.

BONITA.

You may be killed if you go. [*She rises and comes in front of table.*

DENTON.

And if I didn't go, I could never look you in the eyes again. Don't turn away. We may march to-morrow. If I stayed behind, wouldn't you—even you—despise me ? [*He comes near her.*

BONITA.

Go. [*She gives him her hand, but as he takes it she sways with faintness.*

DENTON.

[*Sustaining her.*] Bonita. [*She regains herself.*] Does it make such difference to you ?

BONITA.

Will you answer me one question truly ? [*She gently pushes him from her.*

DENTON.

Yes.

BONITA.

When you left the service, why did you come here ?

DENTON.

[*Pause.*] It was out of doors. It was in the saddle.

BONITA.

Why did n't you go to Dunlap's, or to Fraser's ranches ?

DENTON.

[*Avoiding her gaze.*] Oh—

BONITA.

Truthfully.

DENTON.

[*With reserve.*]   Because I wished to be near you.

BONITA.

Why ?   [DENTON *turns from her and does not reply.*]   You had more courage in your uniform, didn't you ?

DENTON.

I had more right.

BONITA.

Do you mean that that was because you were not on my father's pay-roll ?

DENTON.

I mean, Miss Canby, that—[*Pause.*]—that I am here.   That I should have been stronger than to have come.   That I should have ridden, as you suggest, to Fraser's or to Dunlap's.   [*He again turns away, unable to express himself.*

BONITA.

At the Post, on the night of my dance, you told me that you would almost mutiny to be with me.

DENTON.

Yes.

BONITA.

When you first came, I thought you had left the army—because of me.   [*Pause.*]   Pa thought so, too.   And then—[*Pause.*]   You never said anything, and when the old Major-Domo was killed at Wilcox, and Pa gave you his place, I thought maybe you 'd be more like your old self; because, on a ranch, a Major-Domo is really a Captain.   But you still seemed to avoid me—

DENTON.

[*Expostulating.*]   Miss Canby—

BONITA.

And that kind o' hurts a girl's pride.   I wrote to Estrella about it.

DENTON.

About what?

BONITA.

All of it—your silence, your avoidance of your old comrades.

DENTON.

To Mrs. Bonham?

BONITA.

Yes, and Estrella answered—[*Pause.*]—that you were the bravest and most honorable man she ever knew.

> [DENTON *passes her with a gesture of expostulation and goes right.*

BONITA.

[*Following slightly.*]   I know I'm insistent and unwomanly now, but I didn't hunt you, Mr. Denton.   You went out of your way to make me care for *you;* and now, you can't ride to war, and be silent.   Even a girl has some rights.

DENTON.

Why, God help me, I love you.   [*He turns impulsively, abandoning all self-restraint and embraces her.*

CANBY.

[*Outside.*]   All right, Tony, tell us as soon as you can make 'em out.   [DENTON *goes to the dresser.* BONITA *sits right of table.* CANBY *appears in door at back.*]   You see those soldiers?

DENTON.

Yes, sir.   [CANBY *enters, followed by* MRS. CANBY.

CANBY.

On the move, at last.   Means business.   [*He rings a small tap-bell on the table.*]   Like as not, Ma, the Colonel 'll come back a General.   [SAM, *the Chinaman, enters right.*]   Sam, we want you to hurry up lunch.   We 'll ask the officers to eat with us, Ma.

MRS. CANBY.

'Bout all we can do for 'em in this God-forsaken country.

CANBY.

Get up stuff for about—[*To* DENTON]—How many officers do you suppose there are in that column ?

DENTON.

Those are only the four troops from Fort Grant.   Say fifteen officers.

SAM.

Fifteen ?   Lunch ?

CANBY.

Yes, and put a case of champagne in a tub, and chink it full of cracked ice and salt.

SAM.

Yes, sa.   [*He disappears by door, right.*

MRS. CANBY.

I 'll change my dress.   [*She disappears left.*

CANBY.

[*Smiling broadly.*]   Mother 's been itching for a chance at one o' them new dresses.

DENTON.

Mr. Canby.

CANBY.

Major-Domo. [*He comes down left of table.*

DENTON.

Have you ever thought that—anybody around the ranch might get interested in—in your daughter ?

CANBY.

[*After long pause.*] Yes—at times.

DENTON.

Ever thought that—I might ? [CANBY *reaches to his hip pocket ;* DENTON's *hand quickly drops to his revolver.* CANBY *draws a tobacco pouch, and* DENTON *sighs with relief.*

CANBY.

Yes. [*Takes a chew of tobacco.*

DENTON.

Well, sir, I have. [CANBY *nods, walks slowly back of table, keeping his eye searchingly on* DENTON.] Have you any objection, sir ? [*Pause ;* CANBY *shakes his head.*] I—I 've been talking to her. I 've told her I love her—and—and she 's been good enough to admit that she loves me, sir.

> [CANBY *pauses a moment, leans over and rings bell. He then walks deliberately to the door.* DENTON *crosses to left of table, observing him. At the door* CANBY *takes a cup of water from the olla and rinses his mouth.*
> [SAM *enters, right.*

CANBY.

Sam! Bring a bottle of champagne—right now. [SAM *disappears.*

BONITA.

[*Running to him as he comes to the table.*] Oh! Pa. [CANBY *embraces her, with a swing toward the chair left, and comes in front of table.*

CANBY.

Sit down, kitten. Major-Domo— [BONITA *sits.*

DENTON.

Yes, sir.

CANBY.

I 've lived here and sold beef to Government and Apaches for thirty years. [DENTON *nods.*] Lots of 'em have tried to drive herds in here, and steal a march on me, but whenever they reached the Posts or the Agencies, Canby's cattle was usually there ahead of them. [*He strikes the table, emphatically.*

DENTON.

Yes, sir.

CANBY.

Nobody 's made a move in this valley—twenty miles from peak to peak, and two days in the saddle up and down—that I wasn't on.

DENTON.

Yes, sir.

CANBY.

So it 's a pretty safe bet that I 'd tumble to whatever was doin' in this 'dobe corral, ain't it. [DENTON *nods.*

[SAM *brings in a quart of champagne and three glasses.*

"Sam! Bring a bottle of champagne!"

CANBY.

[*To* SAM.]   Open it.   [*Then to* DENTON.]   And you 've
suited me from start to finish.

DENTON.

Thank you, Mr. Canby.

CANBY.

One year, I may make a hundred thousand dollars.   The next,
I may be broke.   [*He takes the bottle from* SAM *and motions him
to go.*   SAM *disappears into the pantry, right.*]   It all depends on
the weather, and Congress.   Give us plenty of rain, and a tariff
that a Mexican heifer can climb over, and we 're all right.
[*Hands a glass of wine to* DENTON.]   God has charge of the rain.
[*Hands a glass to* BONITA.]   Blast me, if I know whose department the tariff 's in.   Well, here 's luck.   [*They drink.*]   My
boy, up to this time you 've been on a salary.   Now, you 're a
half owner.

DENTON.

Mr. Canby.

CANBY.

I 've just been waitin' for you and Bonita to get together.   [*He
places his glass on the table and walks right.*

DENTON.

[*Sadly.*]   I can't stay, sir.

CANBY.

[*Slowly returning to the table and putting an arm around*
BONITA.]   She 's told you she loves you, and you 're goin' just
the same ?

DENTON.

I must.

CANBY.

[*Persuading.*] The other girl, Estrella, had half a million when she married, and this one hasn't got any the worst of it.

DENTON.

'Tain't money, sir. My old messmates at the 'Cademy are going with their lives. It may be kind o' silly to you, but the flag to which I was taught to take off my hat, that 's going, too.

CANBY.

And damme, if I had twenty years off my shoulders, I 'd go myself. [*To* BONITA.] How is it, kitten, we send him, do we ?

BONITA.

[*Faintly.*] Yes.

CANBY.

Bully ! Go get that finery.

DENTON.

Finery ?

CANBY.

Your old first Lieutenant shoulder straps. *I* cut 'em from your jacket, and *she 's* sewed on an extra bar of braid. [BONITA *gets a cavass coat from the wall.*] Now, brand him a Captain of Arizona Volunteers.

DENTON.

Not this coat. [BONITA *helps him put it on.*]

CANBY.

Yes, let 's see how it looks. [*Passes wine.*] You might 'a' been with these Regulars, but your 're doin' the next best thing—and you go heeled. Yes, sir, you go half owner of the fattest ranch in Arizona. [CANBY *drinks.* BONITA *gets close to*

DENTON, *and both drink from the same glass simultaneously.*]
Now, lad, come back a colonel if you kin. I say that for
Bonita, because, as far as she 's concerned, there 's only one sand-
storm ahead of you. [*He crosses to the door left.*

DENTON.

What 's that, sir ?

CANBY.

Mrs. Canby.

DENTON.

Mrs. Canby ?

CANBY.

Yes. Ma don't care a heap about leather, but she loves gold
braid. There 's hardly anything in the world she won't trade
even for a string of soldier buttons.

DENTON.

'M.

CANBY.

[*Moodily.*] She fixed up Estrella's match with the Colonel.
That wasn't my kind, and now, well—they ain't much more 'n
speakin' to each other.

DENTON.

Too bad ! I thought them most devoted.

CANBY.

They were. The trouble, whatever it is, is since you 've been
here. [TONY *appears at the window.*

TONY.

Governor ! Governor !

CANBY.

Well, Tony ?

TONY.

The soldiers comin' in sight plain enough now.   Colonel 's
with 'em.

CANBY.

The Colonel ?

TONY.

And Mrs. Colonel, too.   [*He disappears.*

BONITA.

Estrella ?

CANBY.

Well, let 's meet 'em, kitten.   [*He goes out the door.*

BONITA.

[*Running to door and stopping.*]   Will you go, too ?   [DENTON
shakes head; she returns and gives him both her hands.]   Harry,
Pa has given you half the business.

DENTON.

He has given me all the world.   [*He kisses her.* BONITA *runs out.*

DENTON.

[*Reflectively.*]   Colonel and wife estranged.   Hardly worth
my silence.   No matter, this is worth it.   [*Looks about.*]   Freedom,
action, the wide horizon.

[SAM *enters from pantry.*

SAM.

May' Domy.   Boss says fifteen—fifty ?

DENTON.

Fifteen—lunch for fifteen.   [*Sam removes bottle and glasses.*

SAM.

Velly good. [*A bugle sounds in the distance.*

DENTON.

[*With suppressed enthusiasm.*] Left into line. Conley's bugle. Not another trumpeter like him in the service. [*The bugle sounds again.*] By jove!

SAM.

[*Smiling.*] You like sodga trumpet, May' Domy?

DENTON.

Like it, Sam? That's a soldier's cocktail. [*Again the bugle.*] Dismount.

SAM.

You sabe what he say, eh? [*Another call.*

DENTON.

Yes, that's the water call.

> [ESTRELLA *and* BONITA *enter;* BONITA *has a rose in her hand.* ESTRELLA *comes silently to* DENTON *and takes his hand.* BONITA *crosses to where* SAM *is, near the dresser.*

BONITA.

Sam, what about luncheon? [*They talk apart.*

ESTRELLA.

[*To* DENTON.] I'll never forget your awful sacrifice for me. Night and morning I prayed for you.

DENTON.

Mrs. Bonham.

ESTRELLA.

Yes, and I've kept my parole. [*She gives him her hand.* SAM *goes out.* BONITA *rejoins them.*

BONITA.

[*Fastening the rose at* ESTRELLA's *throat.*]   How do you think he looks, Estrella?

ESTRELLA.

Looks well—and happy.   I hope you are happy, Mr. Denton?

DENTON.

I 'm the happiest man in the world.   [*He crosses playfully, catching at* BONITA, *who retreats.*

[*The* COLONEL *and* CANBY *pass the window, talking. They appear in the doorway.   The* COLONEL *is travel-stained and dusty.*

COLONEL.

[*As they enter.*]   I really haven't time.   [*He pauses as he sees* DENTON.

CANBY.

[*Noting this.*]   Got a little of the military ourselves—Mr. Denton, my Major-Domo, Captain 1st Arizona Volunteers.

COLONEL.

[*With reserve.*]   Oh—Captain Denton.   [*Bows.*

DENTON.

Colonel.

CANBY.

Why, what 's the matter?

DENTON.

You gentlemen must care to talk together.   I 'll be excused. [*He goes out.*

CANBY.

Why !   Thought you were the best of friends.   [LENA *comes from the pantry with some dishes.*

ESTRELLA.

Why, Lena, how do you do ?

LENA.

Oh, Mrs. Bonham. [*She takes* ESTRELLA's *hand and kisses it effusively.*

ESTRELLA.

Nonsense !

COLONEL.

[*Observing the dishes.*] Here, what 's this for ? We can't stop. [LENA *returns to the pantry.*

CANBY.

Now, why not ?

COLONEL.

Because this is simply a halt to water, and tighten cinches. Our cars are on the side track now. Wouldn't mind a bottle of beer.

CANBY.

Got some champagne on ice, and—

COLONEL.

Beer !

CANBY.

[*To* BONITA.] Beer. [BONITA *leaves to fetch it.*

ESTRELLA.

And I 'm to stay here, Pa, with you—and Mother—and Bonita.

CANBY.

Of course—I 'll send some champagne to the officers. [BONITA *brings the beer.*

COLONEL.

Coffee's better for 'em. [*Takes beer.*]   Good !
  [MRS. CANBY *re-enters in gaudy costume. She and* ESTRELLA *embrace.*

ESTRELLA.

I 'll send them the coffee.

MRS. CANBY.

Estrella—

ESTRELLA.

I 'd rather, Mother.   I 'm at home, now, for a while.   [*She goes into the pantry.*

  [*The* DOCTOR *and* MISS MACCULLAGH *enter.*

CANBY.

[*In exaggerated welcome.*]   How are you !   [MRS. CANBY *also greets them.*

BONITA.

[*To* MISS MACCULLAGH.]   You goin' to stay with us, too ?

MISS MACCULLAGH.

No, dear.   [*Displays Red Cross insignia.*

CANBY.

Quit school teachin', eh ?

MISS MACCULLAGH.

Yes, for good.

DOCTOR.

Colonel—

MISS MACCULLAGH.

Doctor Fenlon, if you don't like suspenders, wear a belt, please.

DOCTOR.

[*To* COLONEL.] That two-story, next to Major Cochran's, at the Post—

COLONEL.

Yes. [*Pause, during which* DOCTOR *looks at* MISS MACCULLAGH.] What of it?

DOCTOR.

The custom 's been to assign those 'dobe quarters to the married men. Three bachelors in that.

COLONEL.

No married men unprovided for?

DOCTOR.

[*Shaking head.*] Was wondering what your policy would be if other married men should—turn up when we come back. [*Glances meaningly at* MISS MACCULLAGH.

COLONEL.

Why, oust the boys, of course.

DOCTOR.

[*Smiling reflectively.*] Er—Colonel—

COLONEL.

Well?

DOCTOR.

You 're a member of the Officers' Club?

COLONEL.

Rather.

DOCTOR.

[*To* MISS MACCULLAGH.] He 's the President.

MISS MACCULLAGH.

Why, I know that.

DOCTOR.

[*To* COLONEL.]   Whenever there 's a little game of draw, you usually take chips ?

COLONEL.

Yes.

DOCTOR.

We play pretty much same kind of game ?   Don't hold 'em too close, and, on the other hand, don't bet every dinky ten-spot. [COLONEL *nods.*]   And in the long run, what 's been *your* losses?

COLONEL.

Think I 'm a little ahead.

DOCTOR.

[*To* MISS MACCULLAGH.]   There !   Me, too.

CANBY.

What 's he talkin' about ?

DOCTOR.

[*To* COLONEL.]   Hates it.

MISS MACCULLAGH.

Poker ?

DOCTOR.

Yes.

MISS MACCULLAGH.

I do.

DOCTOR.

[*To* COLONEL.]   See ?

COLONEL.

Not quite.

DOCTOR.

It 's really the only game I care for. [*Turns to* MISS MAC-CULLAGH.] So there 's your explanation.

MISS MACCULLAGH.

What explanation ?

DOCTOR.

This is the third time she 's declared her intention of quitting school, always in my hearing, and she 's displayed a personal interest in my wearing apparel, that nothing short of matrimony can make legitimate.

MISS MACCULLAGH.

Why, you horrible creature !

DOCTOR.

[*To* COLONEL.] But if I can't draw and fill occasionally, what 's a two-story 'dobe to me ? [COLONEL *smiles.*] So that explains my silence. [*He turns to* MISS MACCULLAGH.

MISS MACCULLAGH.

Which is infinitely easier to explain than your speech. [*She goes haughtily out.*

DOCTOR.

My method—healthy irritation. Next time, I 'll ask her directly. She was born for a hospital.

[HODGMAN *enters. Like all the other soldiers of this act, he is dust-covered.*

HODGMAN.

[*Saluting.*] Colonel. Ready in fifteen minutes.

COLONEL.

Good.   [*Returns salute.*]   Governor.   [*Goes to door with*
CANBY.

MRS. CANBY.

I 'm sorry there 's got to be war, but it 's good to see you
again, Captain.   [HODGMAN *shakes hands with* BONITA.

HODGMAN.

Thank you.

BONITA.

Does the army miss Mr. Denton very much, Captain ?   [*The*
COLONEL *goes*.   CANBY *comes down*.

HODGMAN.

Does the army miss Denton ? [*Laughs*.] Oh, not particularly.
The army 's conscious that he 's gone, and it 's rather glad.

BONITA.

Glad ?

HODGMAN.

Pardon !   I forgot that Denton was something of a favorite
with you, Miss Bonita.

MRS. CANBY.

Not at all, Captain.   But, why glad he 's gone ?

HODGMAN.

Rather a dangerous man to have around.

CANBY.

Quick on the trigger ?

HODGMAN.

No.   Denton 's specialty was the ladies.   [*Laughs*.]

CANBY.

Get out !

BONITA.

I don't believe you.

MRS. CANBY.

Bonita !

HODGMAN.

[*With dignity.*] Sorry to brush Miss Canby the wrong way, but—

CANBY.

But about Denton ?

HODGMAN.

[*After a look toward the door for the* COLONEL.] That was why he had to resign.

MRS. CANBY.

[*Looking at* CANBY.] Had to resign ?

CANBY.

Why, had to ? How ?

HODGMAN.

Excuse gossip. [*Laughs.*] But since my veracity is questioned—[*Looks at* BONITA, *then to* MRS. CANBY.]—an officer coming home unexpectedly, found his young wife with another—man. That man was Denton.

BONITA.

That's a falsehood, a cowardly falsehood! [*The women look at* DOCTOR, *who is by the door.* HODGMAN *laughs and crosses to the dresser, right.*

DOCTOR.

First I've heard of it.

CANBY.

You understand, Captain—er—Denton 's my manager here on the ranch.

HODGMAN.

[*In some alarm.*]   Here !

BONITA.

[*Noticing* HODGMAN's *discomfort.*]   I told you it wasn't so.

DOCTOR.

On the place now ?

CANBY.

Yes.   [*The* DOCTOR *goes out in search for* DENTON.

MRS. CANBY.

Who was the woman ?   Mrs. Cochran ?   [*She crosses eagerly to* HODGMAN.

HODGMAN.

[*Leaving her.*]   I can't mention names, Mrs. Canby.

CANBY.

[*As* HODGMAN *passes him.*]   But the fact ?

HODGMAN.

The fact I know.

[ESTRELLA *and* SAM *enter from pantry with big coffee-pot.*

ESTRELLA.

Now, take that to the officers, Sam.

HODGMAN.

[*Overhearing.*]   Coffee ?   I 'll show Sam where to go. Come.

[*He goes out.* SAM *follows.* BONITA *bursts into tears and falls on table.*

ESTRELLA.

Why, little sister, what is it? [*She puts her arms around* BONITA.

MRS. CANBY.

It all comes o' Canby's havin' a punch eat with us.

CANBY.

A Major-Domo ain't a puncher.

ESTRELLA.

Mr. Denton?

MRS. CANBY.

Yes. She thinks she's in love with him, and you know who stubborn a puppy love can be.

CANBY.

Well, Mother, I don't call it puppy love.

BONITA.

[*Looking up.*] If to love once and for always is puppy love, then my love is that. He is the first man I have ever cared for— I am the first woman he has loved. [*She buries her face in* ESTRELLA'S *gown.*

ESTRELLA.

[*Comforting.*] A soldier's sweetheart mustn't cry, Bonita.

MRS. CANBY.

[*Resenting* ESTRELLA'S *attitude.*] We understand there were some didos down at the Post, that Denton had to resign on account of.

ESTRELLA.

His resignation was a mistake. Denton committed no wrong. He is an absolutely upright, innocent man. [*She comes down, indignantly.*

BONITA.

[*Rising and embracing her.*]   Estrella!

ESTRELLA.

And you love him, darling, all you know how?

MRS. CANBY.

[*Dominantly.*]   You may think he's innocent, Estrella, but you can't *know* anything about it.

ESTRELLA.

I *can* know, and I *do know*.

CANBY.

[*Apprehensively.*]   How, daughter?

ESTRELLA.

Because at the time of which he was accused—[*Pause.*] Denton was with me.   [CANBY *and wife exchange looks.* BONITA *recoils from* Estrella.

BONITA.

With you?

ESTRELLA.

With me.

MRS. CANBY.

Where?

ESTRELLA.

[*Puzzled.*]   Why, in my drawing-room.   [*Pause.*]   What is the matter?

CANBY.

Did—did the Colonel find you there?

ESTRELLA.

[*Hunted and at bay.*]   The Colonel?

CANBY.

Yes. When you and Denton were together, did the Colonel come in of a sudden and make trouble about it ?

ESTRELLA.

With whom have you been talking ?

BONITA.

Captain Hodgman.

ESTRELLA.

[*Hysterically.*] My God ! To my own people ! What a poltroon ! [*She weeps.*

[*The* COLONEL *re-enters followed by the* DOCTOR.

COLONEL.

Goodbye. Don't cry about it. [*He avoids* ESTRELLA's *extended hand.*

ESTRELLA.

Frank—Don't humiliate me here, however you distrust me.

COLONEL.

Where did you get that rose ? [*He looks at the rose on her breast.*

ESTRELLA.

Bonita put it there. Will you have it ?

[CANBY *goes into doorway at back. The* DOCTOR *talks apart with* BONITA *and* MRS. CANBY.

COLONEL.

No—[*Pause.*] Denton is here.

ESTRELLA.

Yes.

COLONEL.

Did you know it?

ESTRELLA.

Yes.

COLONEL.

That is why you asked me to bring you.

ESTRELLA.

No, I didn't want to be at the Post while you were gone. Frank! Don't smile in that bitter way; don't let these people know that you hate me.

COLONEL.

[*In undertone.*] My God! I love you with a perverseness that makes me despise myself.

ESTRELLA.

And I love you. There was never a thought between me and Denton, I swear it.

COLONEL.

We can't talk of it now.

ESTRELLA.

It's been two months—and—

COLONEL.

Yes—two months in hell. Don't talk of—it—now.

ESTRELLA.

Come a minute with me, Frank. [*Pause. She goes out left; the* COLONEL *follows.*

CANBY.

Poor girl, I don't blame her; Colonel 'd be a pretty easy mark for the fever.. [*He comes inside.*

DOCTOR.

Oh, I 'll get some suspenders, and then Miss MacCullagh can look after the Colonel.

[SERGEANT KELLAR *enters.*

KELLAR.

The Colonel here?

CANBY.

Be right out. How are you, Sergeant?

KELLAR.

Mr. Canby, I haven't seen you since my Lena—is—here.

CANBY.

Oh, that 's all right, Sergeant.

KELLAR.

I never forget it. But you have been fader for two girls, you know how a man's heart is for one. And I think about your care for Lena. [*To* DOCTOR.] Dat is so, Doctor, you know. [*To* CANBY.] She is here, yet?

CANBY.

Oh, yes.

KELLAR.

Good girl, now?

CANBY.

Splendid girl.

KELLAR.

Mit de men—is behave all right?

CANBY.

You bet. The best vaquero on my place is dead in love with her.

KELLAR.

Yes?

MRS. CANBY.

Wants to marry her. I'll find him. [*She goes in search of* TONY.

KELLAR.

Lena likes him?

CANBY.

Yes, I think so.

KELLAR.

German?

CANBY.

No, he's a Mexican, but a pretty good one. Going to Cuba with our volunteers.

KELLAR.

Well—[*He looks around at* BONITA.

CANBY.

Coming now.

KELLAR.

I talk mit him. [*Again looks at* BONITA, *who, seeing his anxiety, goes out by pantry door.*

CANBY.

[*To the* DOCTOR.] You don't have to build a fire under her, do you? [TONY *appears at window*

TONY.

Yes, sa. [*Sees* KELLAR.] Sergeant.

CANBY.

Come in. [TONY *leaves the window.*

KELLAR.

Is dis man? [TONY *appears in doorway and comes in, followed by* MRS. CANBY.

CANBY.

That 's Tony. [*Pause. Men regard each other in panic silence.*

TONY.

What is the matter ?

CANBY.

The Sergeant—

KELLAR.

Mr. Canby tell me—that Lena is—that maybe you like Lena.

TONY.

[*Firing up.*] Lena ? Is my own beezness. For him, I rope the cow. What I think, what I lofe, is no beezness, but there— [*To heaven*]—and me. [*He slaps his breast and breathes hard.*

CANBY.

[*Soothingly.*] Well, keep your shirt on, Tony. Ain't anybody kickin'.

> [LENA *enters and shrinks back into doorway of pantry.*

KELLAR.

Der—ah—Mr. Canby speaks fine for you. If Lena shall like you, I am glad. But I don't want some man to like Lena, und den some day find out. It is right de man must know before I go vay—now !

CANBY.

Well, I think he does.

KELLAR.

Yes ! [*They look at* TONY.

CANBY.

You know—er—Lena—about the trouble Lena had ?

TONY.

[*Angrily.*] Yes—yes. I know.

CANBY.

Yes, he knows.

KELLAR.

[*Leading him.*] And still—yet?

TONY.

[*With spirit.*] What the difference? Some say I marry her. First she tell me his name—and then—[*Pause, and successful effort at self-control.*]—Never mind. Now—now she—lofes me. [LENA *covers her face.*

CANBY.

[*Answering* DOCTOR's *look.*] That's Arizona. We're a little shy on water, but there's as much charity for a woman as you can round up in the Gospel of St. John. [*He signals* TONY *to go.* TONY, *going reluctantly, bows.* KELLAR *salutes him.*

KELLAR.

Vare is Lena? [TONY *pauses..*

CANBY.

In the pantry, likely. [*He starts down and sees her.*

KELLAR.

[*Turning.*] Lena. [*He embraces her and turns helplessly to* CANBY. CANBY *points off.* KELLAR *goes with* LENA *into the pantry.* TONY *tries to follow, and is stopped by* CANBY.

TONY.

Is my beezness—I go dere ! [*Pause.* CANBY *slaps him on the back.* TONY *follows* LENA *into pantry.*

"Is my beezness—I go dere!"

CANBY.

[*Turning to* DOCTOR.] Eh? [DOCTOR *nods,* " You bet."

DENTON.

[*Meeting* DOCTOR *at the door.*] Why, hello Doctor. Good of you to ask for me.

DOCTOR.

[*Effusively.*] Denton! And those? [*Points to shoulder-straps.*

[BONITA *re-enters hurriedly by door at back.*

DENTON.

Volunteers.

BONITA.

[*To* CANBY.] Ask him now. Before Captain Hodgman goes.

CANBY.

Oh—er—Mr. Denton—[DENTON *attends; pause.*] Captain Hodgman said something here, that you ought to know 'bout 'fore you go. It 's about your leavin' the Cavalry.

DENTON.

Well?

CANBY.

What was the reason?

DENTON.

What did Hodgman say?

CANBY.

[*Pause.*] An officer's wife. Was that it?

DENTON.

[*Pause.*] I can't explain just now.

DOCTOR.

Excuse me. [*He goes out.*

CANBY.

Now.

DENTON.

Not now, sir.

CANBY.

You mean 'cause the women are here?

DENTON.

No sir.   The truth concerns another more than it does myself.

CANBY.

[*Pause.*]   Er—a—Captain Denton.   [*Pause.*]   You know I —er—[*Pause.* BONITA *goes to* CANBY, *who puts an arm about her.*] We take a man on here, and ask no questions.   We know when he throws his saddle on his horse, whether he understands his business or not.   He may be a minister backslidin', or a banker savin' his last lung, or a train-robber on his vacation—we don't care.   A good many of our most useful men have made their mistakes.   All we care about now is, will they stand the gaff? Will they set sixty hours in the saddle, holdin' a herd that's tryin' to stampede all the time?   Now, without makin' you any fine talk, you can give anyone of 'em the fifteen ball.   I don't know whether it's somethin' you learned in the school, or whether you just happened to pick the right kind of a grandfather, or what.   But your equal has never been in this territory in my time.   [BONITA *kisses her father.*

DENTON.

You're very good, sir.

CANBY.

All of which is merely to say that my proposition about half owner will still go—after you do explain your leaving the Cavalry —if the explanation doesn't hit too near home to me.

DENTON.

Very well, sir.

CANBY.

And if it *does* pinch any woman that I 'm due to protect, why—I 'll protect 'em all right.

DENTON.

I hope so.

CANBY.

You know whether you want to talk or not, but until you do, we copper the daughter proposition.

DENTON.

You mean you withdraw your consent—concerning Miss Bonita.

CANBY.

That 's it.

MRS. CANBY.

[*With antagonism for* DENTON.] Why? Had you given it?

CANBY.

I had—and if the boy squares himself, Mother, *you* kin buck all you want to. It goes as it lays.

DENTON.

I 'll square myself. I—blundered into a false position trying to help a friend, but before I 'll give up the woman I love, or even hurt her by any doubt, I 'll tell—I resigned because I—[*Stops and breathes hard, with effort at control.*

BONITA.

[*Crossing to him.*] Captain Denton—I don't doubt you. [*She gives him her hand ;* CANBY *restrains* MRS. CANBY *from interfering.*
[KELLAR *comes quickly from pantry door.*

KELLAR.

[*In suppressed·excitement.*]   Lieutenant !

DENTON.

[*With melancholy.*] Oh Kellar, how are you ? [*Takes his hand.*

KELLAR.

I have seen my Lena.

DENTON.

What 's the matter ?

KELLAR.

She will marry Tony. She tells me and Tony de man's name. A tamnt loafer ! I got even if dey hang me for it.

DENTON.

Steady—steady, old man.   [HODGMAN *re-enters.*

KELLAR.

[*Seeing* HODGMAN.]   Oh, I can't stand it !

CANBY.

[*Coming between* DENTON *and* HODGMAN.]   Here 's your authority. Captain Hodgman, Captain Denton, Arizona Volunteers and incidentally my partner in the cattle business. [*To* DENTON.] Need me ?

DENTON.

[*With gesture to* CANBY, *but eye on* HODGMAN.] Please go, sir.

"Ask him now!"

CANBY.

Go on, Mother, kitten. [*He puts women out and follows them.*
[HODGMAN *goes left.*

HODGMAN.

[*Defiantly.*] Well? [DENTON *regards* HODGMAN *a moment, then steps near to him. After a moment's pause he strikes* HODGMAN *in the face with his sombrero, at the same time drawing hi. revolver.*

HODGMAN.

[*Recoiling.*] Sergeant Kellar.

KELLAR.

[*Saluting.*] Captain.

HODGMAN.

Arrest this man. [TONY *appears in the pantry door struggling with* LENA, *who is trying to restrain him.*

KELLAR.

[*Saluting.*] I'll see you damned first!
[TONY *fires*; DENTON, *startled by the noise, accidentally fires his gun into the floor*; HODGMAN *falls*; TONY *disappears.*

DENTON.

[*Turning to* KELLAR.] Kellar!

KELLAR.

I didn't shoot him.

COLONEL.

[*Entering.*] What's that firing? Why, Captain—
[CANBY *enters.*

HODGMAN.

[*Pointing accusingly.*]   Denton.

CANBY.

[*To* DENTON.]   You shoot him ?

DENTON.

No.

COLONEL.

[*Grabbing* DENTON'S *revolver and quickly examining it.*]   An empty shell, and it 's hot.

DENTON.

. Discharged by accident.

[*Enter* HALLOCK, DOCTOR, *some troopers and cowboys.
Enter* MRS. CANBY.

HODGMAN.

[*Apparently dying.*]   Denton struck me in the face.   I told Sergeant Kellar to arrest him.   Kellar refused.   Denton shot me.

[DOCTOR *kneels by* HODGMAN.

COLONEL.

Mr. Hallock, put these two men under guard.

[*There is a murmur of opposition and threatened rescue
by the cowboys.*

DENTON.

[*Restraining them.*]   Hold on, boys !   [*The cowboys obey him.*

HALLOCK.

[*To* KELLAR *and* DENTON.]   Fall in.   [KELLAR *and* DENTON
*march out under arrest, amid a chorus of exclamations and ques-
tions from the cowboys.*

CURTAIN

THE FOURTH ACT

HE scene is the same as that of the first act. Twenty minutes are supposed to have elapsed since the end of the third act. COLONEL, LIEUTENANTS HALLOCK *and* YOUNG, CANBY, BONITA *and* MRS. CANBY *are in the courtyard. An orderly is at the gate.*

COLONEL.
Tell Major Cochran to keep those volunteers outside the fences.

HALLOCK.
[*Saluting.*]   B troop deployed in that duty now, sir.

COLONEL.
[*Briskly.*]   Very well.   My compliments to the Major, and tell him to keep 'em there.   Get the rest of the regiment ready to move.

HALLOCK.
Yes, sir.   [*He salutes.   The* COLONEL *returns the salute.* HALLOCK *goes briskly out.*

CANBY.
[*Angrily.*]   The men from this ranch want their horses.

COLONEL.
They can't have 'em.   They 've shown a disposition to make

trouble and I 'll keep 'em away from the stables till we go. Mr. Young—

YOUNG.

Colonel. [*Salutes.*

COLONEL.

[*Saluting.*] Ask Doctor Fenlon how Captain Hodgman 's doing.

YOUNG.

Yes sir. [*Salutes and goes briskly into the dining room.*

BONITA.

Colonel Bonham.

COLONEL.

Bonita—

BONITA.

That guard won't let me speak to Mr. Denton.

COLONEL.

My orders.

CANBY.

Why ?

COLONEL.

I don't want anybody to see either of the prisoners.

CANBY.

Well, ain't that a little high-handed with one of my men ?

COLONEL.

Call it anything you want to, Canby, but you know better than to buck against the cavalry, don't you ?

CANBY.

I ain't looking for any trouble, but when anybody puts my ranch under martial law, I 'm goin' to holler some. ·

COLONEL.

Well, holler. [YOUNG *re-enters from the dining-room.*] How is he?

YOUNG.

[*Saluting.*] Doctor Fenlon is probing for the ball. See you himself in a minute.

CANBY.

[*Apart to* MRS. CANBY.] If he wasn't Estrella's husband—

BONITA.

Mr. Young.

YOUNG.

Miss Canby.

BONITA.

They 've got Mr. Denton in the blacksmith shop, under guard. Will you take him a letter for me?

MRS. CANBY.

You won't send any letter to that man, Bonita.

CANBY.

Well, hold on. I reckon one commanding officer 's enough, Mother. [*To* BONITA.] You write your letter.

BONITA.

It 's written.

CANBY.

Then give it to Mr. Young.

MRS. CANBY.

[*Warningly as the letter is passed.*] Bonita!

CANBY.

[*Interposing.*] Mother.

MRS. CANBY.

[*Sharply.*]   Am I under martial law, Henry Canby?

CANBY.

[*In same tone.*]   No, but you ain't sellin' any too high in the pools.

YOUNG.

[*Extending letter.*]   Colonel?

COLONEL.

No.

YOUNG.

Sorry, Miss Canby.   [*Returns letter.*

CANBY.

[*Getting out his pocket-book.*]   Give me the letter, Bonita.

BONITA.

Here.

CANBY.

[*Licking a postage stamp and fixing it to the letter.*]   There! There's a two-cent stamp on it.   Now I reckon the United States mail is about as big as the Eleventh Cavalry.   [*Starts toward the gate.*

BONITA.

Splendid, Paw.

CANBY.

I'll deliver the letter myself.

MRS. CANBY.

Henry Canby.

CANBY.

Well, Madam?   [*He turns in the gateway.*

MRS. CANBY.

If you carry that letter to him, I put my bonnet on.

CANBY.

You do?

MRS. CANBY.

I do. We 've had our understanding. It 's no fault of mine that these two offspring was girls, but they are girls, and they 're in my department.

CANBY.

But here 's a letter with a United States brand upon it. The government buys my beef, and bonnet or no bonnet, Mother, I 'll put this in the right corral. [*Starts.*

COLONEL.

[*In tone of command.*] Canby.

CANBY.

Well?

COLONEL.

Don't be a fool. I 've got twenty minutes in which to make an investigation, and turn Denton, or some other guilty man, over to the civil authorities with the facts. Every attempt of his friends to hamper that, will react against him.

CANBY.

Well, make your investigation.

COLONEL.

I 've had no chance. Your punchers are menacing, and taking my attention. I don't want to destroy them, but we 're getting where a half hour is worth more to us than their lives, and, I 'm sorry to say, more than yours.

CANBY.

But fair play—fair play.

COLONEL.

In what?

CANBY.

Your trial.

COLONEL.

Bring in two of Denton's company to hear it.

CANBY.

Now you're talking.

COLONEL.

[*To* YOUNG] Go with him. [YOUNG *and* CANBY *go out of gate and go left.*] Orderly, ask Major Cochran and the commissioned officers of A troop to come here. [*The orderly salutes and goes out of the gate and to the right.*

DOCTOR.

[*Coming from dining-room.*] Haven't finished, Colonel. Have given him stimulant, and we're only waiting.

COLONEL.

Found the ball? [*His tone is business-like and brisk.*

DOCTOR.

Located, but no use to extract it. Too painful, unless we use chloroform, and he wouldn't rally from that.

COLONEL.

What are his chances!

DOCTOR.

None.

COLONEL.

Positively none ?

DOCTOR.

Positively none. [ESTRELLA *comes from the house.*

COLONEL.

Then get the ball.

[*The* DOCTOR *salutes and goes, followed by the* COLONEL.

BONITA.

Will he die, Colonel ?

COLONEL.

Surgeon says so. [*Disappears with* DOCTOR.

ESTRELLA.

Bonita.

BONITA.

Do *you* think he shot him ?

ESTRELLA.

I don't know.

MRS. CANBY.

[*Severely.*] Was there any reason why he should have shot him ?

ESTRELLA.

Yes.

BONITA.

Ah !

ESTRELLA.

But not between Denton and me.

BONITA.

Why, then ?

ESTRELLA.

For the lie that Denton cared for me.   Of all the men in the world, Hodgman knew that was a lie.

BONITA.

Estrella—Estrella !   [*She looks anxiously into her sister's face, insisting on the truth.*

ESTRELLA.

[*Convincingly.*]   Little sister, yes.   [BONITA *goes to her.* ESTRELLA *embraces* BONITA.

MRS. CANBY.

[*Unrelenting.*]   But Hodgman says he shot him, and the Doctor says Hodgman 'll die.

ESTRELLA.

Die ?

MRS. CANBY.

Yes.

BONITA.

[*Anxiously.*]   What can they do to Denton ?

MRS. CANBY.

Well, what do you think they 'll do ?   You was born here.

BONITA.

Oh, if I were only a man.   [TONY *comes from the stable.*

MRS. CANBY.

That wouldn't count much with a jury.

BONITA.

[*Quickly.*]   Tony—

TONY.

Señorita.

TONY

BONITA.

They 're going to give Major-Domo up to the Sheriff at Tucson.

TONY.

Not by damn sight.

BONITA.

They will try.

TONY.

[*Melodramatically.*] Before they get by Tucson, one hundred vaquero stops him.

MRS. CANBY.

Now, see here, Tony, no devilment.

BONITA.

Maybe you won't have to wait for that. Maybe some chance will happen for him to get away from here.

TONY.

[*Eagerly.*] Yes!

BONITA.

[*Suggesting.*] If he had my horse—

TONY.

Cochise !

BONITA.

Yes, Cochise.

TONY.

Ah! [TONY *kisses his finger tips in an imaginary farewell.*

BONITA.

Put Major-Domo's saddle on him.

TONY

[*Turning to go.*] Yes—yes, Señorita. To hell with Fort

Grant soldiers.   You tal me, I rope the Colonel he self.   [*Goes into stable high in hope.*

MRS. CANBY.

Now, Bonita, whenever you 've done with your highfalutins, we 'll get back to earth.   Mr. Denton 'll take his chances with the law, same as any other man that gets too gay with his gun.

BONITA.

[*Fatefully and with folded arms.*]   Let 's don't talk about it, Mother.

[MAJOR COCHRAN, *a Captain and two Lieutenants enter the court.*

MAJOR COCHRAN.

[*To* ESTRELLA.]   The Colonel sent for us.

       [*The* COLONEL *enters.   The officers salute him.   The* COLONEL *returns their salute.*

COLONEL.

Orderly!   Tell the Sergeant of the Guard to bring Sergeant Kellar and Captain Denton in here.

       [*Orderly salutes and goes out left.*

MRS. CANBY.

Colonel.

COLONEL.

Mrs. Canby.

MRS. CANBY.

You might as well know there 's a petticoat plot to rescue Mr. Denton.

      [COLONEL *looks at* ESTRELLA.

BONITA.

It 's mine.

COLONEL.

Oh!

[LENA *enters from house.*

BONITA.

[*Going to* COLONEL.]   Colonel.   [*Pause.*]   I 've always tried to be friends with you.

COLONEL.

I 'm sure of that, Bonita.

BONITA.

And this isn't a time to mince matters, or for a girl to play at being shy.   I love that man you 've got under guard, and any advantage you take over him, is one you take over me, too.   I feel just that way about it, and any chance you give him, or fair play, goes double.   Understand ?

COLONEL.

Perfectly.

BONITA.

If war 's on, I guess your regiment 'll get enough trouble, and this one man needn't keep you sitting up nights.

COLONEL.

Bonita—I held Denton on my knee when he wasn't larger than that.   If he 's got a show on God's earth, it 's with me. [*Pauses impressively, then offers* BONITA *his hand which she takes in evident gratitude.*

[CANBY *and two cowboys enter.*

CANBY.

Who saddled Cochise ?

BONITA.

Done for me.

> [*The* GUARD *with* DENTON *and* KELLAR *enters and halts at command.*

LENA.

Father ! [*She impulsively starts to* KELLAR *who is about to embrace her.*

COLONEL.

Stand back. [KELLAR *comes to attention.* LENA *shrinks back rebuked.*]   Major Cochran and gentlemen, as you know, Captain Hodgman was shot in that room, about half an hour ago.   He says Captain Denton shot him.   I 've asked you to meet me in an inquiry into the facts, which, of course, must be brief.   These men of the volunteers and Mr. Canby are here, as friends of the prisoner.   I 'll ask Mr. Hallock to take notes of our work, and you men will attest them.

> [HALLOCK *goes to table.*   TONY *appears with* BONITA'S *horse at the gate.*

COLONEL.

Ready ?

HALLOCK.

Yes sir.   [*Prepares to write.*

COLONEL.

[*With a paper.*]   This is Captain Hodgman's statement, which he hasn't the strength at present to sign.   [*Hands it to* CANBY.]   It affirms that Captain Denton, 1st Arizona Volunteers, struck Captain Hodgman, 11th United States Cavalry, in the face with his hat, and without any retaliating blow from Hodgman, shot Hodgman.   *I* entered the room, myself, at the sound of a revolver.   [*To* HALLOCK.]   Write this—And placed Captain

Denton and Sergeant Kellar—Kellar of 11th United States Cavalry—under guard. Kellar's daughter, Lena, was also there. I took Denton's weapon, which is here—[*He takes a revolver from the table.*] Colt's Army 44, chamber under hammer empty, barrel warm from recent discharge. Tag it, Mr. Hallock, and mark it Exhibit A on tag and also in your minutes.

HALLOCK.

[*Looking about.*] Have no tag.

COLONEL.

[*Impatiently.*] Take the back of that writing tab. [*Tears pasteboard back into two pieces and throws them on the table.*

CANBY.

I 'm through with this. [*Returns* HODGMAN'S *statement to* COLONEL.

COLONEL.

Captain Denton ! [TONY *leaving the horse in care of a cowboy, quickly approaches* DENTON *and whispers to him.*

DENTON.

[*Stepping down two paces.*] Denial. [*Pause ; then speaks slowly that* HALLOCK *may report him.*] Did strike him with my hat. The shot came from some one else to my right, to Captain Hodgman's left. I had my revolver in my hand. The start of the report to my right gave an involuntary pressure to my trigger, and I fired. As Hodgman fell, I turned to Sergeant Kellar, thinking *he* had fired, but his hands were empty.

[TONY *comes unobtrusively down left.*

COLONEL.

You admit striking Captain Hodgman ?

DENTON.

I do.

COLONEL.

Why?

DENTON.

[*Pause.*]   A personal matter.   He had lied about me to my employer, I might say, my partner in business.

CANBY

Partner in business—is right.

COLONEL.

What had he said? [*Pause; to* HALLOCK.] Declines to answer.

CANBY.

[*To* DENTON.]   Answer!

COLONEL.

The man has that right.

BONITA.

[*Advancing.*]   Answer, Captain Denton.   [*Pause; then impulsively.*]   He told my father, and me, that Captain Denton was forced to resign from the regular army—

DENTON.

Bonita!

COLONEL.

[*To Hallock.*]   Don't write.

BONITA.

Because of another man's wife.   [*Pause.*

MRS. CANBY.

He said your wife.

[ESTRELLA *sinks to her knees and covers her face.*

COLONEL.

[*Calmly.*]   Then he did lie.

BONITA.

I knew it !   Estrella !   [*Goes quickly to* ESTRELLA *and puts her arms about her.*

COLONEL.

Sergeant Kellar.   [KELLAR *advances two paces.* DENTON *retires the same.*]   Did you see Captain Denton shoot Captain Hodgman ?

KELLAR.

No, za.

COLONEL.

You were present ?

KELLAR.

Yes, za.

COLONEL.

Watching the man ?

KELLAR.

Yes, za.

COLONEL.

And you didn't see him shoot ?

KELLAR.

No, za.

COLONEL.

Why not ?

KELLAR.

[*Pause.*]   I looked 'round.

COLONEL.

Why ?

KELLAR.

[*Longer pause.*]   Dere was a noise behind.   I looked 'round. Lieutenant Denton—

C O L O N E L.

[*To* HALLOCK.]   *Captain* Denton.

K E L L A R.

[*Correcting himself.*]   Captain Denton say "Kellar!"   I say
" *I* didn't shoot him."

C O L O N E L.

What was the noise behind you ?   [*Pause. Then more sharply.*]
The noise behind you, what was it ?   [*Pause.   Now angrily.*]
Answer ?

L E N A.

It was me.

C O L O N E L.

[*Regretting the development.*]   Your daughter, Lena ?

K E L L A R.

[*Slowly.*]   Yez, za.

C O L O N E L.

[*Annoyed. Consulting* HODGMAN's *statement, and resuming inquiry
with increased severity.*]   Captain Hodgman says he had previously
ordered you to arrest Captain Denton.

K E L L A R.

[*Quickly.*]   Yez, za.

C O L O N E L.

That you refused ?

K E L L A R.

Yez, za.

C O L O N E L.

Why ?   [KELLAR *hesitates.*]   Why ?

K E L L A R.

[*In a burst.*]   He was a damned loafer.   My Lena—he
ruined her—ruined her—my Lena !

COLONEL.

What ! [*There is a general movement among the spectators.*

KELLAR.

Yez, za—by Gott in Himmel—if de whole army kills me.
[*He struggles a moment for self-control, then stoically folds his arms.*

COLONEL.

Did *you* shoot him ?

KELLAR.

No.

COLONEL.

The noise that distracted you—was it a gun shot ?

KELLAR.

[*Pause.*]   Yez, za.
    [*All eyes are now upon* LENA.

COLONEL.

From—behind—you ?   [*Pause.*

HALLOCK.

I 've written—"from behind him."

COLONEL.

And when you turned, your daughter, Lena, was there ?

KELLAR.

[*Slowly.*]   Yez, za.
    [DOCTOR FENLON *comes from the dining-room, his coat off and sleeves rolled up.*

COLONEL.

[*After pause.*]   Well ?

DOCTOR.

The ball. [*Hands a bullet to* COLONEL *and returns to dining-room.*

COLONEL.

[*To* HALLOCK.] Mark exhibit B, ball extracted from Captain Hodgman's breast, by Dr. Fenlon; calibre of ball, 38. [*Pause.*] Mr. Denton your revolver is 44. [*Picks up revolver.*] I release you. [*Cowboys in gateway yell and wave their hats. There is an answering yell from outside, accompanied by shots.*

DENTON.

[*Advancing.*] Thank you. My revolver. [*Extends hand.*

COLONEL.

Is part of this record. Take mine. [*He hands his own revolver to* DENTON *who takes it, with some show of emotion.*

COLONEL.

[*Pause.*] Lena Kellar.

KELLAR.

Lena. [*Starts impulsively toward her.*

COLONEL.

[*Fiercely.*] Attention. [KELLAR *comes to attention.*] Lena, do you know who fired this shot?

CANBY.

One minute, Colonel.

COLONEL.

The girl must answer or decline to answer.

CANBY.

That's just what I want her to know. If her answer would

any way go against her, she can keep still. [TONY, *standing to the left of the others, calmly strikes a match and lights a cigarette.*

COLONEL.

Do you know who fired this shot, that struck Captain Hodgman? [*Pause.*] Declines to answer. [*Pause.*] Did you shoot him? [*Pause.*] Declines to answer. Did you know Captain Hodgman? Had you any motive for injuring him, or wishing him injury? [*Pause.*] Declines to answer. [*Pause.*] Lena—as you were the only person present at the time of this shooting, as your father testifies that you had cause of complaint against Captain Hodgman, as your silence indicates you are in possession of facts concerning the shooting, if you did not actually commit it, I must place you under arrest, and turn you over to the civil authority.

KELLAR.

[*Aspirantly.*] Gott!

TONY.

No! [*Sullenly and coming to the centre of the group.*

COLONEL.

Do you know anything of this?

TONY.

[*Pause.*] I shoot him. [*General movement of surprise by the listeners.*] My gun thirty-eight. She will be my wife—Tony Mostano. [*He tenderly embraces* LENA.

COLONEL.

[*With relief.*] That simplifies everything.

CANBY.

And with an Arizona jury, it's a cinch.

COLONEL.

Major Cochran, detail four men to take this vaquero to Tucson.

MAJOR.

Yes, sir.   [*Is about to go.*

TONY.

One minute.   [*On signal from* COLONEL *all wait.*]   While he [*Pointing to* HALLOCK.]—is here, I tell you.   I was in the kitchen; these men are thare.   [*Diagraming it on stage.*]   Hodgman, damn him! is *there.*   Lena tells me this is the man.   I look in the door so.   I pop him—bang!   I jomp back.   [*Suiting his action to the word,* TONY *jumps back and vaults on to the horse, starting off at a gallop.*

COLONEL.

Stop him.   [*The cowboys close the gates, while affecting to rush out of them.* TONY'*s horse is heard galloping away, cheered by cowboy yells outside.*

COLONEL.

Open those gates.

CANBY.

Why, certainly.   [*Slowly drags his men away and opens the gates.* MAJOR COCHRAN *and the* GUARD *rush into gateway.*

MAJOR.

He's through the line.   Shall they fire?   [*The guard is at "aim."*

LENA.

[*Frantically.*]   No.

COLONEL.

No.   Pursue and arrest him.

　　　　[MAJOR *salutes ond exit.   Orders heard rapidly outside ; then sound of several pursuing horses.*

MRS. CANBY.

Well, I never!

BONITA.

[*Exultantly.*]   He was on Cochise.

CANBY.

Yes, and they—they won't any troopers catch him.

COLONEL.

That 's all, gentlemen.   Get ready for march.   Sergeant Kellar, pending inquiry, reduced to ranks.   [KELLAR *goes out much depressed.*]   Send those minutes to Sheriff—copy to Department.   [*To* HALLOCK.

HALLOCK.

Yes, sir.   [*Takes his notes and goes out of gate, and to the right.*

COLONEL.

Denton, I 'm glad this officer's death will not be at your door. [DENTON *bows.*]   Orderly, my horse.   [*He goes into the dining-room.*

ESTRELLA.

Mr. Denton.

DENTON.

Mrs. Bonham.

ESTRELLA.

I want to speak with you and the Colonel before he goes.

BONITA.

What is it, Estrella.

COLONEL.

[*Coming quickly from the house.*]   Mr. Canby, Captain Hodgman cannot live.   I 'll leave a detail to wire his people, and consult their wishes.

CANBY.

Yes, sir.

MRS. CANBY.

And, Colonel—

COLONEL.

Yes.

MRS. CANBY.

You said he lied. [*Pause.*] Did he? [*Searchingly.*

COLONEL.

The cause of Mr. Denton's resignation was not that given by this dying officer. Captain Denton, I want you to believe I 've never spoken to any one on earth concerning the facts connected with your resignation.

DENTON.

I *do* believe that.

CANBY.

What *was* the real cause for Denton's leaving? I ask it in his presence, because he has asked to marry my daughter, Bonita.

COLONEL.

It was a matter personal to him, and of which I will not speak.

CANBY.

If it was any nonsense with Estrella, *I* want you to say so.

COLONEL.

It—was—not—that.

CANBY.

Tell me, too, that it was nothing against his honor—nothing that should make the little one ashamed for loving him. [*Pause.*] She 's the sister of your wife, Colonel Bonham. *I* ask you to answer.

COLONEL.

Her sister knows all of the circumstances that I know. Bonita's happiness more nearly concerns her than it does me. She will have to tell you. Goodbye. [*He starts away.*

ESTRELLA.

Wait, I *will* tell them and you shall hear me. [*The* COLONEL *pauses and returns.*] My husband did find Mr. Denton in our drawing-room—and—I was there, too. I was going away—Denton came to prevent us. He took from Captain Hodgman my jewels, which I had given him, and which were all of *me* he loved, and told him to go. Then I heard my husband returning. In that terrible moment, I knew that I loved my husband, and I hoped to keep him from learning the truth. I made Mr. Denton go back of the curtain, but Captain Hodgman met my husband on his way and told him that Denton was in the house. My husband discovered Mr. Denton, guiltily hiding, as he thought. He had him searched—and found—my jewels—and a letter from Captain Hodgman to me, planning our flight. Sergeant Kellar hid the letter. The jewels seemed the explanation of Denton's presence, and, without believing his own words, my husband called Mr. Denton a thief, and demanded his resignation. Oh, Denton, I thank you with all my broken heart! But it was all in vain. From that day my husband has distrusted *me*—not you. He knew you couldn't steal, and he doesn't know that I love him. And I am punished as only women can understand.

> [*Kneels at table weeping. The rose which* BONITA *gave her drops from her throat to the stage.* BONITA *instinctively starts toward* ESTRELLA, *but* CANBY *restrains her.*

CANBY.

[*Going to* ESTRELLA's *side.*] Gentlemen, from the minute they put on long dresses, I reckon every father fears that a moment like this may come to *him*. We 've been uncommon proud of Strella, and Ma and me have throwed out our chests and stepped high. It seems she 's mixed it up a little now, but they ain't any trouble comin' to her that her Gov'nor ain't goin' to divide. [*He lifts her up and folds her close to his breast. Pause.*] I know that it 's your say, Colonel, and I can see you 're turnin' it over in your mind. I *want* you to do that, and do *all* of it, before you talk *any*.

[*Pause.* HALLOCK *re-enters.*

HALLOCK.

[*Saluting.*] Colonel, ready. [COLONEL *answers salute and starts to 'go.* BONITA *interposes, with tearful vehemence.*

BONITA.

Colonel Bonham. You must speak to my sister!

COLONEL.

[*Pause.*] Tell Major Cochran to start. I 'll overtake you.
[HALLOCK *salutes and goes.*

BONITA.

[*Continuing, almost hysterically.*] You never danced with her. You never took her to the towns. You were always at headquarters. Don't put all the blame on her.
[*There is the distant sound of a bugle.*

COLONEL.

[*To* DENTON, *with an effort at judicial calm.*] The letter that was on you when Kellar arrested you—

BONITA

DENTON.

[*Taking his tone from the* COLONEL.] Kellar returned it to me, and I sent it back to Mrs. Bonham.

ESTRELLA.

[*Lifting her face from her father's shoulder.*] I have it.

COLONEL.

You first got it, how ? [*To* DENTON.

DENTON.

From Kellar. Lena had given it to him. [COLONEL *looks at* LENA.

LENA.

I saw Captain Hodgman give it to Mrs. Bonham, and I took it.

DENTON.

[*Pause.*] I have reason to believe that, after that night, Mrs. Bonham never spoke to Captain Hodgman again.

COLONEL.

[*Pause.*] Mr. Canby—[*Pause.*]—I do not care to say anything that I may wish unsaid. I must join my regiment. I—I will leave—*Mrs. Bonham* in your care—till I return.

ESTRELLA.

Frank—[*Pause ; she slowly approaches him.*]—you 're not a young man any longer. There will be fever as well as war. You may not return.

COLONEL.

Worse fates than that may come to a soldier. [*He turns to* DENTON.

ESTRELLA.

I must say more to you.   [*She shrinks, hurt by the rebuff, and*
CANBY *quickly takes her in his arms again.*   MRS. CANBY, *moved
by* ESTRELLA'S *suffering, crosses to her.*

COLONEL.

[*Taking* DENTON's *hand.*]   My boy.   [*Pause.*]   Your father
and I—on the same horse—bang into Miles's dining-room—
[*There is something in his voice very like weakness.*

DENTON.

I know.

COLONEL.

We 're both going to the front.   I 'll wire the department,
and you 've got to rejoin the 11th.

DENTON.

Why, Colonel—

COLONEL.

[*Insisting.*]   If it 's only for one week.   You will give an old
man that chance of reparation.

DENTON.

Yes—[*Pause.*]—and you—give the wife a chance?   [*The*
COLONEL *makes a momentary effort at composure, and approaches*
ESTRELLA, *whom* CANBY *pushes gently toward her husband.*

ESTRELLA.

Frank—I love you.

COLONEL.

And—this man, who is dying?

ESTRELLA.

No—never.   It was a madness, a recoil from the dreariness of the desert—a woman too much alone. [*Pause.*] Can't you say one kind thing—one word of—forgiveness?

> [*The* COLONEL *lifts his head; the look on his face softens to tenderness. He is about to speak, when there comes a second and more distant sound of the bugle.*

COLONEL.

When—I—come—back. [*He starts away.*

ESTRELLA.

[*Taking one step after him.*] Frank—[*She turns back to* CANBY'S *ready embrace. The* COLONEL, *hearing her sob, stops and looks back. The others move in an involuntary gesture of appeal. He signals silence; comes to where the rose which* ESTRELLA *wore is lying and stoops to get it.* CANBY *quickly turns* ESTRELLA'S *face so that she sees her husband pick up the rose and thrust it into the breast of his blouse. He goes.*

CURTAIN